P9-CDK-426

Andrew Curtis

About the Author

BETH LORDAN is the author of the novel *August Heat* and the short story collection *And Both Shall Row*. Her short fiction appeared in *The Best American Short Stories 2002*, *The Atlantic Monthly*, and *Gettysburg Review*, as well as on NPR's *Selected Shorts*. The recipient of a Creative Writing Fellowship from the National Endowment for the Arts, as well as an O'Henry Award for her short fiction, Lordan teaches fiction writing at Southern Illinois University at Carbondale. She lives in Carbondale, Illinois, with her husband.

ALSO BY
BETH LORDAN

And Both Shall Row: A Novella and Stories

August Heat

BUT COME YE BACK

A NOVEL IN STORIES

BETH LORDAN

Perennial

An Imprint of HarperCollinsPublishers

"The Man with the Lapdog," "From Mutton Island," "Digging," and "Penumbra" originally appeared in *The Atlantic Monthly*. "Evening" originally appeared in *Book Magazine*.

This book is a work of fiction.
The characters, incidents, and dialogue are drawn from
the author's imagination and are not to be construed as real.
Any resemblance to actual events or persons, living or dead,
is entirely coincidental.

A hardcover edition of this book was published in 2004
by William Morrow, an imprint of HarperCollins Publishers.

BUT COME YE BACK. Copyright © 2004 by Beth Lordan.
All rights reserved.
Printed in the United States of America. No part of this book
may be used or reproduced in any manner whatsoever without written
permission except in the case of brief quotations embodied in critical articles
and reviews. For information address HarperCollins Publishers Inc.,
10 East 53rd Street, New York, NY 10022.

HarperCollins books may be purchased for educational,
business, or sales promotional use. For information please write:
Special Markets Department, HarperCollins Publishers Inc.,
10 East 53rd Street, New York, NY 10022.

First Perennial edition published 2005.

The Library of Congress has catalogued
the hardcover edition as follows:

Lordan, Beth.
But come ye back : a novel in stories / Beth Lordan—1st ed.
    p. cm.
    ISBN 0-06-053036-7
    1. Americans—Ireland—Fiction. 2. Irish Americans—Fiction.
3. Married people—Fiction. 4. Ireland—Fiction. I. Title.

PS3562.O73B88   2004
813'.54—dc21

2003056217

ISBN 0-06-053037-5 (pbk.)

05 06 07 08 09 ❖/RRD 10 9 8 7 6 5 4 3 2 1

FOR MY HUSBAND,
ANDREW CURTIS

ACKNOWLEDGMENTS

The author gratefully acknowledges the indispensable support and assistance of Dr. Charles Fanning, Director of Irish and Irish Immigration Studies at Southern Illinois University Carbondale, and the Irish students of that program; the Illinois Arts Council; Norah Lovern and her family; Molly Edwards and her family; Lisa Bankoff, her agent; and Claire Wachtel, her editor.

BUT COME
YE BACK

CEMETERY SUNDAY

On the moving day itself, everything went beautifully, straight on from the moment Mary woke to a sliver of bright July sunlight under the hotel-room drapes with the idea that this whole undertaking was courageous. The extravagance of the thought tickled her, and she grinned, listening to Lyle's steady breathing, but why not? The last time she and Lyle had carried labeled cardboard boxes upstairs and stacked them in uncurtained rooms, their boys had been small, and they'd been moving from near Boston to near Cleveland, and she'd believed then she'd never move house again. And yet here they were, Lyle at sixty-five and she at sixty, having sold that house and posted their belongings across the ocean to start, again, a new home, in Galway, the town of her childhood.

She and Lyle had been back in Galway only two days, just long enough to get adjusted to the time difference, but they'd been over last summer to choose a house, and she'd written and telephoned, and her sister, Róisín, had given advice, and everything was arranged. All those belongings (the best bed linens and table linens and crockery, the photo albums and special Christmas ornaments, the childhood presents and homemade cards from the boys, and—in the bottom of a box marked MARY—WINTER, with a few things that had been her mother's—the old necktie box containing her own plait, cut off when she left Ireland thirty-four years ago to marry Lyle), all those cherished things she needed to make a home, sat in boxes in a storage locker, to be brought in by Róisín's grandson Barty in his truck. Róisín's husband, Michael Carey, would go with him and oversee; since his heart attack last year, he wasn't allowed to lift, and Barty, with his earrings and all, wasn't a boy to send without supervision, Róisín herself said. The furniture Mary and Lyle had chosen last summer was to be delivered this same morning, and Lyle would supervise all that unloading and setting up. Mary and Róisín would direct the boxes and keep tea coming.

Mary took the sunshine as a blessing on this brave new life, and she let nothing in the day shake her from it. When the men from Tom Dempsey's Furniture were late arriving, she said, "Why, now we'll have the chance to dust the moldings before the rooms are filled with things," and when Lyle grumbled, she sent him off to the shop two streets over for the newspaper and bread and tea. "By the time you're back, they'll have your chair in the sitting room," she said, and they did. They were fine lads, too, cheery and strong, and it did her heart good to hear their young voices in the new house (though Lyle went on grumbling as he told them where to put the things they unloaded—"Seems like they'd know the difference between a kitchen table and a coffee table without being told," he said) (and she said back, laughing, "Ah, they do, but they're not so sure an American would agree!").

She thought Lyle was heroic, too, coming away with her to a foreign country where he knew nobody. She'd seldom thought of returning until after their boys were off on their own, but then, when Lyle retired, and more and more of their friends moved away to Florida or back wherever they'd come from, the rare thought had become a wish. Back here, she and Róisín would go about together: they'd talk of their parents and the world as it had been when they were Mary and Róisín Curtin, girls together; they'd share their worries about their grown children. The sea would be near, and butter would have a taste to it, and she'd understand the weather; she'd get to know her brothers' wives, and her brothers, who had still been boys when she left. Lyle had no close family left in America; his father had been from Mayo (though he'd died before Lyle knew him, and Lyle had never made any great claim to Irishness, that foolishness of so many Americans about green beer and claddagh rings). She'd had no family at her wedding and had lived almost forty years far from home for his sake, and she wanted to grow old among her own people and be buried among them in a grave with flowers planted on it and curbing all around.

When she'd finally brought up the subject of moving, she'd been ready to say all that, but it hadn't been necessary. She'd just said she wanted to be near her sister and her brothers, and he had nodded—they'd been eating chicken, she remembered—and said he'd look into it. A week later he'd said it looked like a plan, and for all that he'd explained to her the economic advantages (this fine two-bedroom, semidetached house had cost less than a new condo in Ohio, to say nothing of the moderate climate and the savings on heat, the reasonable approach to health care), she took it as an act of love.

So none of the grumbling he did that moving day touched her at all, and none of the small difficulties made any real bother either. If the box spring rubbed off a patch of paint in the upstairs corridor as the lads turned it at the top of the stairs, take it for a sign: she'd not been so very fond of that grayish white color, and once they were settled in, Lyle might enjoy a project of painting it something brighter. A bit of summer rain never hurt anyone, and if Barty tracked dirt on the carpet bringing in the damp boxes from the truck, well, that's what a vacuum cleaner's for, she said to

Róisín (who laughed—"Vacuum cleaner, is it?" she said, and then, "We say hoover," which sounded funny to Mary, so they both laughed), and it wouldn't be the last dirt tracked there, faith. The little fireplace was so pretty it made no sense to fuss about the fact that if they put the television to the left of the fireplace, the afternoon sun would make a glare on the screen, and if they put it to the right, they'd be squinting into the sun itself at news time. "The sun's uncertain most afternoons," she said, and Róisín said, "Uncertain's not in it," so "There, then," Mary said, "and if it's shining, we might be out in it ourselves."

Even when she came into the kitchen and found Róisín unpacking a box marked KITCHEN—the first of the boxes to be opened by anyone in Mary's new house—she just cleared her throat and noticed instead that Róisín was setting the cups to the right of the kitchen sink for washing, instead of to the left as Mary herself would have done. She thought of asking whether setting them to the left might be the American way, or if it was just personal, but she didn't. All she said was, "Oh, I'd nearly forgotten those blue cups!" and then she found the package of lightbulbs and was heading back up the stairs when she heard Róisín say, "She's a great many cups, I'd say," in a pinching voice.

That voice, from as deep in their girlhood as her own suspicion of insult, did stop her, there on the second step, but only for an instant. Mary could hardly blame her. She did have a great many cups (though she'd not forgotten the blue ones, that Kevin had brought her his first Christmas at college, and didn't know why she'd said it at all)—a great many of everything, it was beginning to seem, for all she'd left behind, and she was glad the house had an attic. In the guest room she clicked the bulb firmly into the pretty blue bedside lamp. The boxes needed unpacking by somebody, and it was kind of Róisín to come and spend her day helping, with Michael hardly cheery about sparing her, if the way he'd gone off without a word had meaning, and the stiffness in her shoulders the damp brought on.

No, Mary held that morning sense of courage and cheer all through the day. The lads from Dempsey's finished and left, Barty got all the boxes in, and the telephone-company man and the television cable man came and went. They had the bed made up and dishes enough unpacked and washed and set in the presses, towels found and suitcases unloaded before Róisín left, late in the afternoon. "I'll ring you tomorrow," she said, "and drive you out to Quinnsworth for a real shopping," and Mary said that would be fine (and then, as Róisín was getting into her car, Mary wondered if she should have kissed her good-bye—so many years since they'd had this casual a leavetaking). The day had come around warm and sunny again; Mary and Lyle walked into town for a supper of fish and chips at McDonagh's, through the crush of tourists enjoying the long light of the summer evening. They were both very tired over their cod, and, without mentioning it, agreed to take a taxi home.

She'd left the light on in the kitchen at the back, a hint of home that gave her a pleasant shiver as Lyle opened the gate and they walked around to the back door. The house wasn't large, even by Irish standards. The former owner had thought to buy the house on the other side of the wall and convert the two to a B&B, but that hadn't happened, so the downstairs remained only the large kitchen and the sitting room and a half bath and laundry room, though upstairs had been changed to the two bedrooms, each with a bath. Their house in Ohio, with its family room and dining room, the study and the four bedrooms and all the rest, had been much bigger—so big, once the boys had grown, that somehow she and Lyle had gotten lost from one another in all those rooms, all that quiet.

Lyle unlocked the kitchen and they went in. Here, in this house, they might find their way to something like who they'd been in the seven years before their boys were born.

She walked through the kitchen, past a stack of boxes (behind her Lyle stopped, shifted a box), and into the sitting room. She stood still a moment in the dusk, and then turned on the lamp beside Lyle's chair.

While they'd been away, walls and floor, corners and angles had taken the weight and contours of the furniture, and Mary saw, in the lamplight, the shape their living here could have. Here Lyle would sit, his newspaper folded in sections on the table beside him; she would carry in the tea and biscuits to this table in the afternoon, and she'd sit over here after she'd poured the tea, and he would tell her what he thought. The fire would flicker there in the evenings and on dark days; they'd come in, first one and then the other, from some chore, and they'd each take up something quiet—a letter, a bit of sewing—and sit together without speaking, easily, listening to the fire. Their sons were grown and not here, and there'd be a little of that sadness, always, as in the first years there had been always that tentative sadness of having no child. She'd come in with a dusting cloth, and glance out the window, and he'd be on his knees in the garden, or just turning to come back in, with crumbs of dirt on his cuffs for her to scold him about. They'd watch something on the television—she'd explain something to him, and he'd make fun of something. Even when she was in the kitchen, even if Róisín called in and they stood out there talking, or had a morning cup of tea at the kitchen table, she'd feel this room close by, with the small sofa, their two chairs, a third for company, the tables and the lamps. She touched the back of his chair, knowing it would take his scent in time. And nights when he stayed up, she'd hear the television through the floor, and know how he sat, hear when he laughed.

"Where the hell is the box of records?"

"Records?" she said, but he didn't seem to hear her, and the temper in his voice rose, and she knew his face was flushed.

"I knew I should have gone with them—they've gone and left half the stuff out there in the storage locker, and you had Barty turn the key back in, didn't you?"

She touched two fingers to her forehead, against the frown, and went back to the kitchen, where he stood with a paring knife in his hand and all four boxes opened. "The box of records," she said, "the one marked 'Study'?"

"I don't know what the hell you marked it, but it's not here." He held up a handful of wadded newspaper to prove his point.

"It's in the guest room," she said. "There's two marked 'Study,' just inside the door. Did you need it tonight?"

"No, I didn't need it tonight," he said, spiteful, and tossed the paring knife into the sink.

"That's good, so—I'm about to go on to bed." She turned from him, an old habit of giving him privacy to recover from his anger, but she could see in her mind every gesture he'd make—he'd smooth his hair with both hands and then pat his palms twice against his thighs as if checking his pockets, and then he'd lift his chin and, with his right hand, smooth his throat in two quick passes.

"I'm not that tired," he said. "You go ahead—I'm going to take a look at the television." She heard the two soft pats.

"Right, so," she said. "Good night, then."

Going up the stairs, she counted four small dents she hadn't noticed earlier in the wall, one of them quite deep. She touched it, and he called up, "If you wanted to, we could go for a walk along the bay after breakfast," and there it was again—the life they would make here: a long walk down the prom with Lyle, he admiring the daylight and the two of them trying to guess who were the Americans among the tourists, the view of Clare if the air was clear, and then home, and, in the cold months, he'd spread yesterday's newspaper on the hearth and shovel out last night's ashes, while she did the washing-up. "Grand," she called back down, "it'll do us both the world of good."

She settled into familiar sheets on the new bed that first night, thinking that she'd never cooked for him in Ireland, and how the smell of the broiling rashers and sausages would travel up those stairs to him in the morning, and how bright the blue cups would look on the table. She thought of their sons, and eventual grandchildren occurred to her; she and Róisín would one day talk about their grandchildren instead of how many cups a decent woman might have, she thought, and so even the small knot of irritation with her sister unraveled, and everything was in place and quite nearly perfect as sleep came on.

—————

By the end of the second week, Mary understood that Róisín had little interest in talking about her grandchildren, although Mary asked after them. Instead, she talked about her joints, her aching joints, to which most topics returned—the weather, of course, but also unexpected things like cheese (which could aggravate inflammation, some said), the Olympics (some of those drugs they abused did wonders, but you couldn't get them), and knitting (no, she'd made no jumpers in years—worst thing in the world for the shoulders). Cemetery Sunday was coming, the day families gathered at the graves of their people and mass was said in the cemeteries, but even when Mary said how glad she was the Galway churches had moved it to August— when they were girls, it had been in November, and the mass had been cold and miserable, but in August people could get a holiday and come back, and she wondered if their brothers would come (thinking to hint that she'd like to host the family lunch, make a kind of housewarming party of it)—Róisín rushed right back to her joints: "They'll come of course—not John, all the way from Australia, but Jamie and Tom, and the wives. The bishop's to do the mass this year, didn't I tell you? He's a lovely priest, and they'll set up the little summerhouse beside the chapel for it. Please God we'll have a fine day. Oh, but here it is only days away and I've nothing done to the graves! What'll they think, Mary?"

"Ah, they'll understand," Mary said.

Róisín gave a bitter little laugh. She'd grown very thin and sharp with age, who had been the slender dancing sister, the one with the hope of beauty. "They expect it of me, they do, Mary, they do—I'm the one still here, you know. I've always done it, or Michael has. But he's delicate now, since the heart attack. I'd do it, you know, I don't mind it at all, tidying and a few flowers, as we've always had, but even in the warm weather, it's my shoulders with no strength in them, and then the pain goes down to the wrists." And then she was off on what the doctor said and how nothing really helped, though she'd a friend swore by herbal teas.

Mary herself, though she'd gotten stout, had never felt more fit, with the walking she and Lyle did now, and the good air, and the sense of new beginnings, and here was Róisín, only a year older, talking like an old woman. Or whinging like a spoiled child, which was a thought Mary wasn't proud of: for all she knew, she'd be in pain herself in a year. So the next morning, as she and Lyle were putting the last of the boxes into the attic, she said, "Would you think Róisín has aged much?"

"Haven't noticed," Lyle said. He was coming up the stairs behind her, carrying a box of special-occasion tablecloths and dishes (pumpkins and Easter chicks and turkeys and fat red hearts, and Mary wondered whatever she'd imagined, bringing them along). "I guess she doesn't look any worse than she ever did."

Mary laughed out loud and then quickly covered her mouth to stop the laugh, surprised by her own quick delight at the possibility of insult to Róisín. Who, after all, was a large part of why she'd wanted to come back—to grow old among familiar people, and no one could be more familiar than her sister, the two of them sharing a bed for the first twenty years of their lives, whatever differences they'd had.

"Pull down the stairs, will you? I'd just as soon get this done," he said, but he'd a grin on his face, too.

She reached up with the stick and fished down the cord. "It's just she's on about getting creaky," she said, and lowered the stairs carefully. "Not complaining, exactly. But on about it. There. Here—I'll hold the box while you go up." He went up three of the ladderlike steps, and she handed him the carton, and he set it above him on the attic floor and then went the rest of the way up himself. "She says she hasn't the strength to keep up her garden or tidy the graves, and here's Cemetery Sunday coming." She peered up into the dimness. "Don't put it next to the tank," she said.

After a thump and a shoving sound, he said, "So what's the problem?" and his heels and bottom appeared, coming down the ladder.

"There's cloth in it, Lyle—if the tank sweats, it'll get

damp and ruined." She shook her head. Sometimes it seemed to her that she was the only one who paid attention to the small details that were the real cause of big problems, for all that Róisín had been considered the sensible one, and Lyle made a big noise of being practical.

"Her gardening," he said. "I don't see how her garden's your problem."

She laughed. "Oh, I thought you meant the linens! Here." She picked a fluff of gray dust from his shoulder. "Now, that's the last of it—are you hungry?" She'd bought a nice bit of smoked salmon and meant to surprise him with it.

"It's that time," he said, and folded the stairs back and lifted the contraption until the spring caught and pulled the whole thing into the ceiling. He stood and glared up at it. "That tank won't sweat," he said. "It's double-walled."

"Ah," she said. He'd worked forty years for a hardware firm and he knew such things. In fact, he'd explained the tank to her in the first place, how having the tank in the attic increased the water pressure to the toilet, which was what made the toilet flush so energetically here.

At the foot of the stairs, he said, "I could see what I can do with the grave."

"Would you then?" Mary said, turning to him, surprised again, for she'd never meant to ask him if he would, but now that he'd said it, she wondered whyever she hadn't asked, or if she'd been meaning to, secret even to herself.

"Why not?" he said, and scowled. "I don't mind helping out," he said, as if she'd accused him.

"I'll tell Róisín you've offered," she said, and did a quick calculation on how long the salmon would keep: he was on the edge of taking offense, and a treat would send him over. "What will I make you for lunch?"

"I'm not fussy. Turkey sandwich'd do me fine," he said, and went to the bathroom to wash his hands.

He would notice the salmon in the refrigerator before the day was over, and he would ask when she planned on having that, but by then he'd be pleased again, having something to plan. And Róisín would be pleased, she thought, and thought, too, that she'd been rather stupid not to have guessed help with the grave was what Róisín was hinting after. She smiled, spreading the mustard he liked: Róisín had always been a whinger, but it was only right that Mary and Lyle should take up some of the work here. So Lyle could tend the grave, and Mary would make the lunch for everybody on Cemetery Sunday, and they'd begin to settle into their place here in her family.

That evening, after Lyle had been to the garden center and then to the shop for graph paper, and after they'd had their supper and she'd done the washing-up, with Lyric Radio playing softly there in the kitchen, she stepped into the sitting room and saw that he'd pulled a table up to his chair and was working with colored pencils.

She stood a moment in the doorway, just for the pleasure of seeing him there in the room, the light as it was, his head bent that way, before she said, "Tea?" He still had a fine head of hair.

"Sure," he said, without looking up.

The radio was playing something she thought might be Beethoven; she left it on as she made the tea and fixed the tray and carried it into the sitting room and set it on the table. Lyle dusted his hand across the paper and held it up for her to see. "They don't have much for flowering plants," he said, "but this might work."

She went and stood beside him, her hand on the back of his chair, and he explained that the blue would be forget-me-nots and the red impatiens, the yellow and brown in the middle just marigolds, but what she saw, even in the paleness of the pencil colors, was how it would look in life, planted and growing there on the Curtin grave—the golden cross of marigolds (Mary's gold, her father had called them), circled with sweet blue and dark red, traced with the delicate alyssum like strands of vivid silver—how it would be solemn and beautiful. She saw, too, there in the lamplight, how his hands were aging, thinning, the knuckles more pronounced, and for an instant she recalled those hands moving gentle and smooth over her skin.

"It's lovely so," she said, though it was little enough to

say, about the gift he'd planned here, for her people, and little enough to say about her gratitude that the two of them were here in this room in this light in this moment, exactly as she had hoped and imagined they might be. Little enough to say about his hands and all she knew of them, and she put her own hand on his shoulder. "It's lovely."

The praise and the caress, as she knew they would, made him gruff, and he said, "It's pretty simple, but they don't have much for flowers that'll look okay by Sunday. It's what now—Wednesday? This should work, if I can get them planted tomorrow."

She stepped back to the table where she'd set the tea things and filled his cup.

"Thing'll end up costing probably fifty pounds by the time you add in the taxi fares," he said. He was that proud of his work, and had every right to be.

"I've promised Róisín to go with her to take some things to the Curiosity Shop in the morning, but I could come with you in the afternoon and help," she said, handing him his cup.

"Let's see what the weather's like," he said. Beneath the saucer, their fingers touched, slipped warm against one another. "What's the Curiosity Shop?" he said.

Maybe Mary only imagined that the touch lingered, and that he, too, savored the lingering, but she turned away before she said, "The St. Vincent de Paul's charity shop," as shy and uncertain and happy as if this were flirtation, or courtship.

She knew it was silly—thirty-five years of marriage and two grown children—but that moment's touch was still warm in her mind the next morning, walking with Róisín back to the car from the Curiosity Shop. She'd half a thought to try to tell Róisín about it, but when she thought of saying, Lyle's a fine one, don't you think? she couldn't imagine what else might be said. So instead she said, "I was thinking this morning of the lunch we had the last time we were here for Cemetery Sunday."

"In '91 that was—six years ago?" Róisín said, as if nobody with any sense would remember a lunch for so long.

But Mary did remember it, everyone around the table, and she went on. "It was at a restaurant, in Salt Hill, I think. You'd planned it so nicely."

"In Salt Hill?" The compliment had pleased her. "I suppose so—the Galleon, that would be. They've good potato cakes there, I remember."

"I wondered if you'd a plan set already for this year," Mary said.

Róisín unlocked the car, and they got in just as a fine rain began.

"We might go there again, since ye liked it—they've space for large parties."

"Well, what about this—Lyle and I were thinking this year we might make a lunch party in our new house," Mary said.

"Oh, but ye couldn't do that, Mary!"

More than forty years ago, on another day that threatened rain, Mary had said, I'm thinking of America, and Róisín had said the same thing in the same voice: Oh, but you couldn't do that, Mary! And now as then, that voice brought such a bitterness into Mary's throat that she had to give her head a shake before she could speak at all. "We'd thought to make it a bit of a homecoming celebration," she said, but her own voice, too, seemed to come from that far past, so flat and stiff.

"Oh, but ye've not the room for this great crowd," Róisín said. "We'll be nearly twenty, I'd say," she said. She started the motor with a little flourish, checked her mirrors. "The boys are bringing a child each, and then there's my lot, with the babies and all. Ye'd never fit them in, Mary," but then, with more sympathy than it deserved, "and they'd never expect it, you know—we haven't done it at home in years and years."

Mary drew a deep breath and stretched her hands in her lap. "I'd not thought there'd be so many," she said.

Róisín pulled out, and they drove along beside the docks. It didn't matter, Mary thought. She'd see her brothers and the wives, and have them back one family at a time. It might even be better that way, really.

"I've been thinking about doing the chips," Róisín said, just at the bottom of Quay Street.

"Chips?" Mary said, imagining potatoes, and, so, the lunch, and that Róisín had somehow decided that her own narrow little house was big enough for the great crowd of them.

"The stone so many are doing now."

"Stone?" Mary said. She hated feeling stupid, and felt, with a swift helplessness, that Róisín meant her to feel exactly that.

"For the grave," Róisín said.

"Ah," Mary said, "for the grave. Well, you needn't worry about the grave—Lyle says he'd be glad to do his bit."

"Marble chips, like—they spread them over—it's tidy looking, and you needn't be at it all the time."

"It wouldn't be a bother," Mary said. "Just some marigolds and such—you remember how Da loved marigolds?—but it's pretty so."

"The chips they've got in colors, too."

"Colors?" The car turned and Mary put her hand on the dashboard to steady herself.

"They've the white, and a green, and blue, and I think a kind of silvery clear one—I don't think there's a difference in the cost."

"Ah, there's no need to go that far—Lyle's got it all fig-ured out," Mary said, and she meant to go on and explain the plan, the cross of marigolds, the circle of blue and red, but Róisín interrupted.

"I've figured it myself, Mary," she said. "There's the weed-ing and replacing of the flowers you and your man haven't thought about—the chips have no need to be redone every season."

"You'd not need to redo the flowers at all again. The stone, I suppose, it's good if you've nobody to keep the grave—"

But Róisín spoke over her. "Up a bit, the family whose son was the great hurler, they've put in the white stone, I think."

"You needn't worry about it at all," Mary said, but again there was Róisín's voice, even louder, "Or it might be the blue—for the young people they often do," and Mary'd no intention of hearing about the hurler, so she raised her own voice a bit to say, "It won't cost you a thing—we've always had the flowers," but at the same time Róisín was saying, "I'll just ring Barty, and he can run out to the place where they've the stone in bags," and Mary, nearly shouting, "Lyle's drawn up a plan, Róisín, and been to the garden center—he's the work put in already," this last coming out clear, alone, at the end.

Róisín took the corner quick and hard in the silence their two voices left behind. "I believe," she said, and took the next corner hard again, "I've put in a bit myself, doing the flowers for almost forty years." They'd come to Mary's street now, now to her house. "And now we'll have the chips." The car stopped.

The smell from the old clothes they'd taken to the shop hung in the small car, and outside, the air was gray.

Mary looked at her house through the windshield. When this moment passed, she saw, this moment of Róisín with both hands stiff on the steering wheel and herself denied their parents' grave, she would leave the car, quietly, calmly, without a farewell, and go through her gate and around to her kitchen door. She would enter her house and close the door and stand listening for a second to be certain Lyle was in the sitting room, and then she'd walk through the kitchen, and in the sitting room she would tell him what Róisín had said.

She would be reminding herself, in case he said it for her, that family was what she'd come back for, but he'd only shake out his newspaper and say, from behind it, "I guess it's her call."

"I guess it is," she'd say, and she'd go back into the kitchen and think to give him the smoked salmon, because just his not saying anything else showed how disappointed he was, how hurt. But when she opened the package, she'd remember that she and Róisín had once, as girls together, gone to see where the salmon was smoked. She'd try to remember the details of that day, but instead she'd remember that Róisín had once given her a cherry-colored jumper that suited her. She'd remember Róisín coming to kiss her, all those years ago now when their mother died. They'd quarreled that day, too, but she couldn't think over what: Róisín had been happy, saying she was to marry Michael Carey at Christmas. Michael Carey, who was now an old man, sick and silent. Not able for tending a grave.

There in the car, with the smell of the old clothes, and the rain beginning to prickle on the windshield, Mary didn't imagine how, on Cemetery Sunday, riding up winding Sean Mulvoy Road in the back of a rattling old taxi, she would be reminded that the dead, even more than the living, settled down in families. She didn't think of how she and Lyle would walk up the path, between the graves and the families of the Coffeys and Conneelys, Hickeys and Griffins and Flanagans, past the little cedar tree, how they'd turn to the right at the grave of Martin and Marie Hynes, and there her people would stand, the Curtins together, beside the grave of their parents. She didn't think of courage at all, but she put her hand on her sister's wrist.

Mary said, "I thought you meant potatoes."

Róisín turned her face to Mary, her eyes still narrowed, suspicious.

Mary gave Róisín's wrist a little squeeze, a little shake. "When you said chips." She let go then, and Róisín raised her hand and pressed two fingers to the center of her forehead, a gesture of their mother's.

"Chips," she said.

The rain came down hard then on the roof of the car, and beneath its noise their laughter was only frail music, but music all the same, music all the same, Mary was still telling herself when she'd hung her wet jacket on a chair in her kitchen and stood toweling the rain from her dripping hair, when she could feel the sorrow thickening in her throat. She spread the towel over her jacket and stood with her hands on the dampness of it. They had laughed. Nothing, really, had changed at all, from the way it had always been. She had nothing to cry over, really: she had wanted to be here, and she was here. This was her life, now: this was her home. She closed her eyes and waited, but no other possibility, no wish or intention, came to her.

When she opened her eyes, Lyle stood in the doorway looking at her, his hands in his pockets, and she'd no idea how long he'd been there.

He looked away, at the window over the sink, and then he said, "I was going to make some tea but I couldn't find the kettle."

She said, "It's just there, by the sink."

"We don't have the regular kind anymore, that you put on the stove?"

"No. Just the electric."

He came into the kitchen and tapped the refrigerator with his knuckles. "I saw you've got some smoked salmon in here—you figure on having that today?"

She nodded. "If you want it."

"Better eat it before it goes bad," he said. He smoothed his hand down his throat. "I won't be able to get those plants in, not with this rain."

"No," she agreed. She'd butter some brown bread to go with the salmon, and make him some tea.

"I guess they'll have to put up with the grave the way it is, for one more year—or do something else."

"I guess so," she said. She turned from him then to fill the kettle. "I could make a salad to go with the salmon if you like." She plugged it in, turned it on. "Róisín was saying she might have marble chips put on the grave."

"That's okay with me. Have we got that brown bread?"

"We do," she said. She would make them a nice lunch—she had some cherry tomatoes for the salad, and two kinds of biscuits, she thought, for after, and she might ask him if he'd a plan for their own garden.

FROM MUTTON ISLAND

Yes, of course, even if it's raining," Mary Sullivan said, "but you must tell me the train, Jimmy," and the noise of the bar he was calling from, across the Atlantic, was as clear as if he were here in Galway, as clear as Lyle's heavy steps coming down the stairs. Some cloud moved on, and a rare brilliance lay across the breakfast things.

"I don't know which train," Jimmy said. "He'll just call you from Dublin, okay?"

"That's fine, then—will you speak to your dad?"

"I'm out of money, here, Mam—tell him hi for me—thanks again," and he was gone.

The sunshine faded, flashed again, and disappeared for the day. Lyle would make a fuss, and Jimmy himself wasn't coming. She'd not seen him in the year since Lyle had retired and they'd come here to live. She had never imagined she'd miss Jimmy so, this steady yearning like a wedge in her chest. And now on the telephone she'd not had a chance to say she loved him or to take care. Still, "Mam," he'd said, his baby name for her—hadn't he?—startling after years of his American "Mom," and she held it.

"How much does he want?" Lyle said.

"He didn't ask for money," she said. She pulled the broiler pan out and turned the bacon. "He's the promise of a job, he said, with a landscaping concern."

"Landscaping." He pulled out his chair and sat down. "He called collect in the middle of the night to say he might have a job mowing lawns?"

"He didn't call collect." She lifted his eggs onto the plate, added the bacon, and put his breakfast on the table between his fisted hands. "He sent you his love."

"Like hell he did," Lyle said, but he put his napkin in his lap and began eating.

She let him eat while she poured his coffee and fried her own egg, but there was no sense in letting it hang too long between them, so when she sat down, she said, "He's a friend coming over."

He kept eating, so she said, "He thought we might show him about."

"I bet he did," Lyle said. "I just bet he did. What else did he think? That we sit around over here with nothing else to do, waiting to show his friends around?"

"It won't be so much," she said, watching her own fork cut into the egg. "Only a few days, and he'll be off to Belfast for the rest of his holiday."

"Belfast! Is he nuts?"

"He's studying something in Irish history. It'll only be a few days he's here." She spread jam on her toast. Lyle would get used to the idea; he'd fussed the same when his own cousin came over last summer, and then he'd been lovely when she came.

"He's not staying here?" he demanded.

"We've the room," she said, which they did: she'd insisted they buy a house with a second bedroom and bathroom, so the boys could visit, but she didn't say anything more. She just waited while he wiped his mouth and left the table, while he put on his coat and hat.

"Not that it makes any damned difference what I think, but when does this all happen?"

"Friday."

"This Friday?"

She nodded.

"That's a hell of a lot of notice—two days." He opened the door. "I suppose this guy thinks he's Irish."

"He may think what he likes," she said, and stood.

"With the name of Gilbert Monaghan, I'd think he'd some connection."

After thirty years with Lyle, she wasn't surprised that he came back from the shop with the newspaper and said that Gilbert Monaghan sounded Protestant to him, and snorted when she said she'd enjoy having a young one to cook for again, and grumbled about the expense when she bought a bit extra in the way of food. But she was surprised, and pleased, when, after lunch on Friday itself, he said, "You ought to make him walk out to Mutton Island," and passed her the newspaper folded to a piece called FINAL WALK PLANNED. The piece explained that the tides were rarely but predictably so extreme that one might walk on dry land to the island, almost a mile out in Galway Bay. This Sunday the walk would be possible, for the last time before construction began on the sewage-treatment plant to be built there.

Mary had a faint memory of a narrow spiral of stone steps inside the abandoned lighthouse. "I might have gone once as a girl," she said, and then, vividly, she remembered the wind as she stood with her sister Róisín on a wall, wishing mermaids from the far water. And a woman—her mother? Aunt Norah?—scolding. A magic thing, an island was.

"Bunch of protesters this time, probably," Lyle said.

Being American, he hadn't joined the long quarrel between people who wanted to save the island and people who wanted the plant, but he'd said more than once that no American city the size of Galway would be allowed to pump its raw sewage into the river and canals, where it would be carried out to sea.

And she'd said back that Galway wasn't an American city, praise be to God, and was growing by leaps and bounds, a different city entirely than the Galway she'd grown up in, and poor as the Irish had been for so long, it was no wonder they'd not tended the plumbing—but she supposed he was right. When the canals got low in the summer, the smell was foul. It couldn't be healthful. Still, it was a pity about the lighthouse, and the pretty island itself.

"Maybe not," she said. "There's a magic to it, I'd say." She tried to imagine Gilbert Monaghan seeing the magic. "We might take him so," she said.

"We?" Lyle said. "You got a mouse in your pocket?"

"You might try it," she said. "It's not so far."

He turned the page.

"Gilbert Monaghan and I, then," she said, smiling, and though he didn't smile, he answered the telephone when the boy rang, and was civil.

"Seven forty-five," he reported when he came back to the table. "Is there any coffee left?"

Mary lifted the thermos, nodded. "Could you tell what he's like at all?"

"No," he said, holding out his cup for her to pump the coffee into. "He was polite. That's enough." He took his cup back, added sugar, and picked up his part of the newspaper again.

They walked to the train station through a light rain that misted Mary's glasses, so when the boy stepped down from the train wearing a green high-school athletic jacket, she saw her son. It was only a moment, a leap in her heart, a flash of light—Gilbert Monaghan indeed! when it was Jimmy himself come!—but in that moment trembled the food she would fix, the talk they would have, the plans they would make. She could feel already his cropped hair (whatever was the boy thinking, all his pretty hair cut to stubble that way!) against her palm; she was already shaping the scolding she'd laugh him home with.

"That's the jacket," Lyle said, without a hint of mischief or pleasure in his voice, and raised his hand. The boy came walking through the crowd in a way that wasn't Jimmy's way, and the jacket changed and became a nylon pullover, so Mary already knew. Still, something in her mind kept on adjusting for these things—couldn't Lyle for once be glad to see the boy? and whatever did he have in that knap-sack that made him walk so?—until the very moment Gilbert Monaghan himself, with three earrings in one ear and the edge of a tattoo showing on the side of his neck, stood before them and introduced himself. Even then, even as she was smiling and saying, "Fáilte—that's Irish for wel-come," her hand wanted to touch his face, to be completely certain.

But the moment was brief, and over nearly as it began, long before they got back to the house. By the light in her own kitchen, she saw that he looked like Jimmy only in his lanky height and his blue eyes. Still, coming from the same part of the country, he had some of Jimmy's ways of talk-ing, and she tried to warm to him. "You'll be hungry, I'd think," she said.

"A little," he said, blushing, "but I could just have some bread or something. I don't want to put you to any trouble."

Mary laughed. "No trouble at all—I like feeding boys. The bathroom's down the hall, and I've some cold supper all ready. Do you like smoked salmon at all?"

"Oh—uh, well, I'm vegetarian," he said, touching an ear-ring, "but it's no big deal—"

So she was glad she'd made a nice egg mayonnaise, too, and she said, "Our Jimmy gave up meat for a time, but he'd still have the fish—it's grand food, Irish salmon. Go on and wash your hands," she said, "and I'll have the tea by the time you're back. You'll be dead for sleep, too, I'd think, with that long trip."

She did have the tea ready and the plate of biscuits (she'd bought extra, so she'd a nice selection, and a few sweets as well, knowing how boys were) waiting on the counter when Gilbert came back down the hall, and he and Lyle sat at the table. "There then," she said, taking her own place, and Gilbert unfolded his napkin on his lap and said, "It looks great, Mrs. Sullivan," and took some slaw and salad and a slice of bread.

"So, Gilbert," Lyle said, "you grew up in the Midwest?"

Gilbert said he had, that his parents had a large farm, and that he had two younger brothers and a married sister.

"And you're in college now," Lyle said.

"Yes, sir—I'll finish next May. I'm doing an interdisciplinary major in postcolonial studies."

"Hmp," Lyle said, but he'd his mouth full of salmon, so it was hard to tell what he meant. Lyle was fond of smoked salmon.

"It's a postgraduate course, I'd think?" Mary said.

Gilbert shook his head. "Undergraduate," he said, "but I'll be applying to grad school next year. Could I have some more of that bread, please?"

"You could of course," Mary said, passing the plate. "It's good bread, isn't it? I get it from An Caca Milis, on Abbeygate. They do all the whole-grain natural things there,

breads and cakes and biscuits. They sell at the market, too—
will I take you to the market tomorrow? It's lovely, it is, all
the stalls of crafts and fresh foods, and someone playing
music?"

"It sounds great," he said.

"She's got plans for you," Lyle said. "That's how she is.
Tomorrow the market, Sunday the walk to Mutton Island.
Last summer when my cousin came over from Chicago, she
wore the woman out—of course, she was here longer than
you'll be." He looked over at the plate of biscuits. "Is there
more tea?" he said.

"There is," Mary said. Gilbert hadn't touched the egg, or
the egg salad, and she thought he must be one of those
strict vegetarians, and wondered how she'd feed him, so she
said, "Will you have another cup, Gilbert, and some biscuits?" and then corrected herself, "Cookies they are—it's a
word I've trouble remembering to change from America,
even with my own boys. I was talking with Kevin, our older
son, just a bit ago, and I said, 'What kind of biscuit was it
you liked so in primary school?' and he said, 'Biscuit?' and I
said, 'Oh, cookie,' and then he said it was the fig bars—he
was mad for them all the time he was growing up—but it
made me a little sad so, remembering how American my
boys are, never having the biscuits of my childhood—they
wouldn't know a Jaffa cake from a Jersey creme."

Gilbert grinned and let her pour him more tea and take

away his plate. "I wouldn't either," he said. "It sounds as hard as keeping the RUC and the UVF and the UUP and the IRA all straight."

"Not so hard once you've tasted them," Mary said. "This is the Jersey creme," pointing, "and this is the Jaffa cake."

He took one of each, still smiling.

"How is Jimmy?" Mary said.

"Oh, he's great," Gilbert said.

"Is he working?" Lyle said.

Gilbert looked blank.

"He said he'd word of something," Mary said. "With landscaping?"

"Oh, yeah—yeah, he said that. It'll be great, you know, working outdoors again. It's been a heavy winter. Yeah, I think he said he'd probably be starting this week." His face tensed, stifling a yawn.

"So you're studying politics," Lyle said.

"In a way—I mean, kind of real broadly, trying to see how the political situation got so . . . so, well, sort of so insoluble."

"They let it go on too long," Lyle said. "It could have been stopped years ago."

Gilbert nodded, but Mary could see, again, his mouth holding in a yawn, so she said, "Time enough for politics tomorrow—the boy's dead for sleep. Will you take him up and show him how the shower works?"

A bit later, both of them in bed in the dark, Lyle said, "Could be worse," and Mary said, "He's grand," and then, after a time, "I wonder does he eat cheese at all," but by then Lyle was asleep.

She asked Lyle at breakfast if he wouldn't come with them to the market.

"I've seen the famous hippie market," he said, and then, maybe because of something in her face, "I suppose we could meet for lunch at Tigh Neachtain's." He wiped his mouth and nodded to Gilbert. "They always have something vegetarian, but it's a real Irish pub—crowded, cramped, smoky. Local color." He chuckled.

"Grand, then," Mary said, and once she and Gilbert were out away from the house, she said, "He goes on some, he does—you mustn't let it bother you."

"Oh, I don't mind," Gilbert said. "Jimmy told me—I mean, he said his dad had strong opinions."

Mary laughed, a little guilty, a little grateful to Jimmy. "He does indeed," she said. They were coming to the corner where they'd have to go straight, up the canal to see the cathedral, or turn and cross O'Brien's Bridge, straight into the market, and see the rest later. She decided to do the market first, but she asked, "Will I show you the cathedral on our way home? It was blessed by Cardinal Cushing."

"Is that the same guy that it turned out had a son in America?"

"No," Mary said. "That was Bishop Casey," and she was grateful that the river was high and loud and the footpath crowded as they crossed the bridge.

The market was a success. Gilbert admired the size of the carrots and parsnips, and the fact that they were still dirt-covered. He talked for a bit with the young man selling Celtic armbands (he was Canadian, they discovered, and had a tattoo around his wrist), and was suitably impressed by the bodhran playing of a redheaded fellow at the top of Market Street. He did eat cheese, he said, and at Sheridan's stall Mary bought three kinds and a loaf of good bread, saying they'd make a picnic of the walk to Mutton Island tomorrow. As they went on, he said the smell from the Middle Eastern food stall almost made him wish he still ate meat. A girl with curly black hair turned and said, "Ah, no—there's no meat to it, love—eat all you want," and Mary laughed at Gilbert's blush. "I'd mind myself—that one's from wild Donegal, probably wild herself," she teased. They might have gone around the corner and seen a bit more of the town, but the rain began again, so they made their way to Tigh Neachtain's.

Lyle was there before them and had taken a snug and ordered her a cup of tea. For a moment, in the pleasant flurry of arrival, Mary loved everything—Lyle for the tea,

Gilbert for liking the market, the pub for having a snug, Ireland for being her home. And then Gilbert said, "I'd better wash up. Where's the men's room?" and Lyle burst out in a loud laugh and nearly shouted, "Outdoors!"

It was of course. The toilets at Tigh Neachtain's were outside, in a covered alley, just the kind of thing about Ireland Lyle loved to mock. "The walls are granite a foot thick," she said. "Would you be running pipe through that?" But later Lyle was on about Gilbert's vegetarian lasagna, which did look and smell like paste.

"They've no experience in vegetarian cooking," she said.

"Except potatoes," Lyle said, "and they overcook that, too."

Gilbert mentioned how narrow the streets were.

"The city's old," she said, "the streets just lanes from medieval times, and the buildings too solid to move."

Lyle laughed. "Cow paths, she means."

The rain was bucketing down when they left, and Gilbert said, "It never does stop, does it?"

"That's how we have the million shades of green," she said, just before Lyle stepped in a bit of dog mess on the footpath, and had his say about dogs running loose.

Over the supper of spaghetti with separate meat, she asked again if Lyle would go along with them tomorrow to Mutton Island, and he said no, he'd no patience for pilgrimages, and Gilbert asked what this Mutton Island was. So Lyle had his say about the sewage situation, and about the artist types who'd fought the treatment plant, and how they also wanted to pass an ordinance banning certain colors of paint on the houses—"Infantile color combinations, they say," Lyle said. She'd have preferred other conversation, but Gilbert seemed to enjoy it, and Lyle was making an effort.

As she was clearing away the dishes, Lyle said, "How old are you?"

"Twenty-two," Gilbert said.

"Legal," Lyle said. "Would you like a whiskey?"

"Sure," Gilbert said, and Lyle took the bottle from the cupboard over the sink and poured two small ones and handed one to Gilbert, who held up the glass, smiled, said "Cheers," and drank it down.

Lyle stared.

"Nice," Gilbert said.

Lyle held out his hand for the glass and poured again. "Sip this one," he said. "It's good whiskey," and he went into the front room.

Gilbert shrugged and smiled at her before he followed.

Still, what happened was her fault. She was putting knives and napkins into the brown Sheridan's carry bag along with the cheese and bread for the picnic, and wondering about the breakfast before the long walk, so she went in after them and said to Gilbert, "Do you eat eggs at all?"

"Just free-range eggs," he said. He said it pleasantly enough.

Lyle didn't take it so. "They have those free-range eggs up at Ward's shop," he said. "They cost more than twice what the others do."

Gilbert nodded. "Sure. On the big farms, they keep the chickens locked up all the time, stimulate them with light, give them hormones, so they get greater production, so they can sell cheaper."

"So your position is that it's more important to protect chickens than to feed poor people," Lyle said, and before Gilbert could respond, he said, "Or maybe it's that the finer moral points properly belong to people with money."

She knew well that mean pleasure in his voice. He was a good man, and she had never understood why he needed to act the bully like this. A hundred times he'd done Jimmy so, and then complained the boy avoided conversation with him. And it was no way to treat a guest, however he'd treated your drink.

But Gilbert said, "The healthiest diet anywhere in the world is the cheapest one. People don't need eggs to get protein. Grains and beans do just fine, without fat or cholesterol. So, yeah—the people who can afford the luxury of eggs ought to be responsible for the morality of egg production."

Lyle nodded, sipped his whiskey. The nod nearly fooled her. She nearly turned back to the kitchen, where the washing-up waited, but then he said, "So you'd agree, then, that the Famine was the moral responsibility of the Protestant landowners."

Gilbert tilted his head. "I'd agree that the Famine might be considered the best thing that ever happened to the Irish," he said.

God in Heaven, Mary thought.

"Would you?" Lyle said.

A holy show there'd be now, and not a thing she could do to stop it: Lyle had brought it on, criticizing everything, and Gilbert hadn't a clue he'd gone far past the mark.

"I would—without the Famine, the diaspora would have been delayed who knows how long. As it was, people emigrated and made better lives than they'd ever have been able to make in Ireland." The poor boy thought it was a conversation, and went on as if it were an examination question he'd learned the answer to. "In 1845 there were eight and a half million Irish, most of them living at the subsistence level; today there's forty-four million Irish Americans, most of them middle class or better—and nobody's counted the Irish Canadians, or the Irish Australians."

"I'd be interested to hear you make that argument in Padraic's pub down by the docks," Lyle said, his voice so dangerously level that Mary could hardly keep from saying

And when have you been in Padraic's? to head off what was coming, even though she knew if she said such a thing he'd never forgive her, true as it was. "There's men down there whose grandfathers didn't emigrate—men who stayed and watched their families die while the Protestant landowners' farms got bigger."

Gilbert shrugged, and took a sip of his drink. "Sure—there's a big romantic investment in the idea that the Irish got screwed by the English. It's part of what keeps every-thing such a mess up North. Even so, it's actually another benefit to Ireland—that sentimental idea is a big part of what keeps tourism high and brings the American dollars in."

Lyle exploded. "The babies buried in Connemara would be happy to hear that!" he shouted, his face gone wild red. "All those people dead of hunger and disease are resting real easy now they know they died for the Celtic Tiger!"

"Well—"

"And the men who broke their backs making the Famine roads—and then watched their children scatter to the four winds—"

Now Gilbert was loud, too, "I'm not saying—"

But Lyle was louder, leaning at him now, shaking his fin-ger at him. "You are! You're saying the English saved the Irish, for Christ's sake—saved them!—by starving them to death, boy! Don't stop now! Don't you want to claim the last hundred years of poverty came out of Irish pigheadedness, too, that they didn't all turn goddamned souper?"

Mother of God.

"I don't even know what a super is," Gilbert yelled.

"Converts," Mary heard herself say, nearly whisper.

"Ah," Gilbert said, the beginning of a grin on his face.

"Starving people," Lyle said. "Starving people preyed on by your good Protestants who wouldn't feed them unless they'd renounce their faith. Sound familiar? Sound profitable? Sentimental?" He stood and drank down the rest of his whiskey. "I think I'll take a walk."

Mary didn't move as Lyle left the room and then the house, but Gilbert did: slowly, in four unhurried sips, he finished his whiskey.

"A long day," she said finally, because something had to be said.

Gilbert put his glass carefully on the small table beside the chair and shook his head, the ghost of a grin still around his mouth. "He gets mad, doesn't he."

"The Famine—" she said, but Gilbert stood up.

"Yeah," he said, and touched his earring. "I am pretty tired."

He was right: it wasn't the Famine at all. Lyle had no more been to the Famine graves in Connemara than he'd been to Padraic's bar by the docks. He'd spent no grief on leaving his own sons an ocean away, and he'd not even done his Easter duty since the boys were grown.

And Gilbert didn't care about the chickens, or the Protestants.

"Oh—hey, I was thinking I'd just go on up to Belfast tomorrow. This friend of mine up there, he said anytime."

"You needn't leave," she said, though he did, of course.

"Oh, I know." His faint grin was there still. "It's just I only have, like, ten days. I need to get the whole picture, you know?"

"The first Sunday train's not until after eight," she said.

"That's cool," he said. "I was thinking I'd hitch. It's safe here, right?"

"If you're careful," she said. "You've a map?"

She slept badly. Lyle came back and up to bed not long before she heard Gilbert leave quietly, when it wasn't yet light. She felt herself between the two of them, and let herself descend again through a wedge-shaped core of darkness, invisible. Late in the morning, far too late for the early mass she loved, she came awake and left Lyle snoring quietly in the bed, dressed, made tea, and started out for the cathedral.

The wind came up cold, shaping her face and head as she

walked, and she'd gone as far as O'Brien's Bridge before she stopped. The cathedral was ahead, that had been a huge construction site when she was a girl here. She turned away, and walked back down the streets to the promenade.

She saw people gathered farther up the bay, but she chose a place where she could make her way down to the sand without climbing over rocks. She walked, skirting the huge hanks of seaweed and the pools of seawater the tide had left. She walked, not thinking, her hands in her coat pockets, the wind at her scarf, and then there she was, stepping from the sand onto the long, tangled grass of Mutton Island. Her feet were wet despite the newspaper's promises. The sky hung gray.

The grass of Mutton Island lay like the enormous locks of some giant woman's uncombed hair. Mary felt it beneath her feet as hummocks, springy lumps and tangled dips, and paid attention so she wouldn't trip. She walked as the others did, following the walls and the shadows of paths worn in the old days by the feet of the long-dead lighthouse keeper and his wife and their children and animals, and she came as the others did through the ungated opening into the lighthouse garden.

Here, inside the wall, the wind dropped away, and Mary stepped into its absence, where others stood in small groups. A man pointed out past the back wall of the garden and said, "That's where they'll put it," speaking of the treatment plant.

A younger man turned and looked back across the bay to the city and nodded. "It'll hardly show, will it?"

"So they say," the first man said, gruff and cautious. They were alike, tall and heavy, facing away from each other. "You want to go in, do you?"

"I do—don't you?"

But the older man didn't answer, and the younger—his son, of course—went on through the low doorway of the lighthouse keeper's house. After a moment the father walked deliberately back out of the garden, into the wind.

That was how they were, men. Gilbert, Lyle, Kevin, even Jimmy. Strange to her, just because they were men.

She stood a bit in the garden. Once carrots had been grown here, and beets and parsnips. Deep in the tangle of grass, the remains of a cold frame rotted, so once, too, an experiment with lettuces had been tried. Certainly there would have been cabbages, a line of pale globes, like the memory of the freshly washed faces of children in the twilight as the lighthouse keeper's wife stepped out of the low kitchen to breathe the chilled wind. Down the slope several women were digging the spent daffodils and putting the bulbs into plastic sacks to carry home, a bit of the island saved.

Sentimental, that was, she thought, or maybe rape of the land, and sighed. She had no idea what any of the men would say about it, and she'd no wish to have a Mutton Island daffodil in her own garden. She had walked to an island, and this was what it was: an abandoned garden dug by strangers outside an abandoned home beneath an abandoned lighthouse, all of it about to give way to a sewage-treatment plant. And that was the whole truth of it, except that she'd two miles of cold, wet walking between herself and her house. No mermaids, dear, she thought, no magic.

But she'd come here, and never would again, so she turned and went through the low, dark rooms of the dead lighthouse keeper's house, out into a small yard, and into the lighthouse. The steps were as she faintly remembered, the whitewash flaking from worn stone in a spiral, and tight enough near the top that if a girl hadn't backed up the steps to let her come, she might have changed her mind and gone back down.

But the girl did back up, laughing, and said, "This is so cool," an American voice, and behind her in the dark stairway a child's muffled voice called, "Up here!" Mary climbed up, and stepped out into the wind on the narrow railed platform.

There before her, spread across the littered, mottled, puddled stretch of ocean floor revealed, walked the Irish, in boots and coats, by ones and twos and fours, with children and dogs about them, some moving slowly out toward the small green island, and some, as slowly, away, back toward the larger island. In the gray light they all looked sharp-edged, and divided by great distances.

Beside her an old man wheezed, and said, "Lovely, ant it." She squinted her eyes so the figures blurred.

Hundreds would cross that sand before the extraordinary tide sighed far out toward America and turned itself back to refill Galway Bay. And it was only this they would come to, only this they would leave.

The old man pointed with the end of a cigarette held between his fingers. "Your man there," he said. "Got his lunch, looks like."

She cleared her eyes and looked, and among the figures just off the island stood a man in Lyle's coat and hat, a brown carry bag in one hand, waving his other arm slowly back and forth in the air above his head. "He does," she said. He'd no more be Lyle than Gilbert had been Jimmy, but she raised her own arm and waved, slow and steady, before she turned, deeply tired, and made her way back down the stairs.

The Man with the Lapdog

Almost every morning, as Lyle was getting ready to take the dog for a walk along the bay, his wife would ask, "Are ye down the prom, then?" They had met and married more than thirty years before in Massachusetts, when she was Mary Curtin and he'd thought her a happy combination of exotic and domestic. At sixty-two, after their life in the States, she still called herself a Galway girl; at sixty-seven, after two years of retirement in Galway, Lyle still considered a prom a high-school dance, not two miles of sidewalk beside the water.

So he would say, "We're going to walk along the bay," and hope she'd leave it at that. When they had first come to Ireland, the exchange had had a bit of a joke to it, but he felt it now as unwelcome pressure. He had no intention of taking up Irish idioms—he'd have felt foolish saying "half five" instead of five-thirty, "Tuesday week" instead of next Tuesday, "ye" for plural "you." "Toilet" instead of bathroom was unthinkable. He called things their real names—"pubs" bars, "shops" stores, "chips" french fries, and "gardai" police.

He didn't love the talk, and he didn't love the Irish people, who always stood too close and talked too fast, and he had trouble, still, understanding what they said. He had frightened and embarrassed himself trying to drive on the wrong side of the road with the steering wheel on the wrong side of the car, and had given it up. He disliked the weight of pound coins in his pocket, and he didn't care for Guinness.

And yet, somewhat to his surprise, he liked a lot about Ireland. He liked keeping the small garden behind their house, the way things simply grew and thrived in the steady, cool dampness. He liked the stone walls that surrounded every yard and separated one person's place from another's. He liked the little coal-burning fireplace in the sitting room. After forty years as an accountant for a hardware chain, he liked living in a place where people went for walks, and he liked going for walks. He liked the dog, a longhaired dachshund, a pretty, girlish little thing. He liked the opinionated newspapers, and he liked being a foreigner.

One day in early March, walking along the bay, he saw a couple he probably wouldn't have noticed among the other tourists if it had been summer. They stood arm in arm looking out over the water, the woman dark-haired and attractive in an unglamorous way, the man thin and frail, apparently very ill. Lyle heard her say, "Yes, County Clare—I'm sure of it," her American accent clear; he nodded as he passed, and they nodded in response. The next day their walks crossed at about the same place, and all three smiled in recognition. That evening something on television about preseason tourists reminded him to say that he'd met an American couple.

"Have you?" his wife said. "Where are they from?"

"I don't know," he said, sorry already that he'd said anything.

She tilted her head as if she were being playful and said, "So did ye talk about the weather, then?"

"Yes," he said. "We talked about the ugly weather."

On the third day, when they met again, Lyle gave the leash the small tug that told the dog to sit and said, "It's a beautiful day, isn't it—good to see the sun again."

Something rippled between the man and the woman and came out as a quick laugh in her answer. "It's glorious," she agreed. "And you're American!" she said.

"I am," he said.

The man, too, seemed amused as he put out his hand in introduction. "I'm Mark; this is my wife, Laura. And we, too, are Americans."

"Lyle," he said. He shook Mark's thin hand. "Are you here on vacation?"

"For three weeks," Laura said, as if three weeks were a long, luxurious season. "And you?"

The dog was sitting patiently. "I'm retired, and my wife is Irish, so we came back here to live a couple years ago."

They said where they were from, and how old their children were, and that this was their first trip to Ireland, long dreamed about, and then Laura reached out and put her hand lightly and briefly on the sleeve of Lyle's coat. "I have to tell you: we'd seen you walking here, and we made up a life for you—"

"We assumed you were Irish, of course," Mark said.

"I suppose it's because everything is so exactly like we expected it to be," Laura said. "The stone walls in the fields when we were coming over from Shannon, the pretty shops, the thatched roofs. We even saw a rainbow our first day here. So we just put you into the picture, the Galway gentleman, and when you turn out to be American, it's quite a joke on us." Her eyes sparkled.

Her eyes were very fine, her face strong; Lyle admired even the simple way she held her dark hair in her fist to keep it from blowing across her face. She was coming into middle age with none of the artificiality of so many American women.

"So I've spoiled your postcard," he said, and all three of them laughed. When they parted, he kept the picture of himself her words had made: his overcoat and hat, his kindly aging face, the tidy small dog, obedient at the end of the leash. And he kept, too, the swift pleasure of her hand on his coat.

They met again the next day and the next, stopping to talk for a few minutes. Lyle would recognize them at some distance by Mark's brimmed hat and the bright shawl Laura wore over the shoulders of her coat. They walked in the mornings, she said, before the wind got too strong, because the wind tired Mark. He had lost his hair, and his face was swollen, but Lyle could see that in health he had been a handsome man. They always walked arm in arm, and she often seemed to be supporting him, more as a matter of balance than of strength, but something in the way they looked together led Lyle to believe that, even before Mark's illness, they had often walked this old-fashioned way, side by side, along streets or through parks. Lyle could almost remember the pleasure of that—the hand a warm pressure in the bend of his elbow, the wrist between his arm and his ribs eloquent and secret, the publicness of the linking.

The next evening his wife asked about his Americans, and he told her they were from Idaho, where Mark taught high school and Laura raised their three teenage children, who were with grandparents for these three weeks.

"A teacher," his wife said, wondering. "An expensive holiday for a teacher, and during the term."

"They have those deals," he said. "Two-for-ones. Off season." They were eating spaghetti, and he watched how she poked around among the strands, looking for something in particular.

"From the States to Ireland, do you think?" she said, doubtful.

"I don't know."

She chewed, and he could almost see her mind shifting. "If they did, Jimmy might be looking into it so."

Jimmy was their younger son, twenty-five years old, without a dollar or a plan to his name. "He might," Lyle said, cautiously.

She went on about fares and connections and then safely into a story her sister, Róisín, had told her of a trip somebody had taken by bus from somewhere in Kerry to somewhere in Clare that sped along, if you counted all the time, at a rate of about six miles an hour. Lyle was relieved: they wouldn't have to talk about buying Jimmy a ticket, or how they weren't exactly rich themselves, or about his life-hating caution and how he'd always favored Kevin, and on and on. He finished his supper and waited for the end of the story, the ritual shake of her head, the "It's a terrible country." Back home she had told different stories about Ireland, ending them with "It's a grand country." Sometimes, now, he'd point this out to her, ask why she'd wanted to come back here if it was so damned terrible. But tonight, as he waited, in the noise of the long details of her telling, he thought of how simply Laura had spoken that morning.

She had asked about St. Patrick's Day, how it would be celebrated, while Mark walked alone at a little distance, stooping unsteadily to pick up small shells. Lyle told her that the parade would be small compared with American parades, the day a quiet family holiday, more like Labor Day than Mardi Gras.

"Maybe we'll try the parade, then," she said, watching Mark's slow progress back. "If it's not likely to be a big crowd. He gets tired."

"Is his recovery expected to be long?" Lyle had wondered for days how to ask, and was pleased at how naturally the question came out.

"Oh, he won't recover," she said. "He's dying."

She put no drama into it at all, not into the words, not into the tone, not into the way she raised her hand against the sudden emergence of the sun. "I'm sorry," Lyle said.

She nodded. "So are we." And then they had stood there quiet, waiting for Mark to come back and for their walks in the opposite directions to continue.

He hadn't told his wife any of that, and now she had passed the end of the bus story and come to something else. "It's not the traveling, I told her, it's the staying that's so dear, and she was saying that that's where the money was, in B&Bs, why the people in Kerry half of them in the summer move into caravans in their own back gardens and let all their rooms to the tourists. I couldn't do that, I told her— you know how I am about motels, sleeping in other people's beds, and it'd be the same thing even worse, having strangers in your bed and then going back to it in October so, knowing they'd been there. I'd be thinking I could feel the heat of those bodies in the mattress." She stood and gathered up the plates and silverware.

There, in something that wasn't quite his mind and wasn't quite his body, he felt the sweet warmth a woman left in a bed, and knew that the shape and smell of the warmth were Laura's. So when his wife asked, "They're at a B&B, I'd think, your Americans," he said back, "Why—are you going to go ask what their damned tickets cost?"

She stopped in her work and stared at him. "That was nasty," she said, but he saw that her eyes were only alert, not wounded.

"Oh, give it a rest," he said, and went into the sitting room and turned on the television and called the dog to his lap.

He discovered by accident where they were staying. The day before St. Patrick's, the rain was heavy, so he and the dog were trapped inside with the smell of damp coal ash and his wife's endless talk about the rain—lashing, she said, coming down in rods, she said, bucketing down, and how she hated rain in her face, she said, and, now, a soft day she didn't mind. But by midmorning the next day, the rain stopped, and he said he was going out. As he was putting on his overcoat, she came with a limp hank of shamrock and knelt on the kitchen floor to tie it to the dog's collar. "That looks pretty stupid," he said.

She patted the dog's head and stood up. "It looks lovely." She had two more bits, and he allowed her to pin one to the lapel of his coat. "Are you thinking of going to the parade, then?" she asked.

"It's not until noon." He hooked the leash onto the dog's collar. "Did you want to go?"

She made a wry face and pushed her hand in the air between them. "It's a poor excuse for a parade," she said. "Róisín's calling by for me to help her with her new curtains. I'll be back before tea."

Out of sight of the house, he stooped and adjusted the dog's greenery. The air was clean and cool. As he passed one of the schools, he could hear a few horns behind the building—kids preparing for the parade. Small family groups were slowly walking toward the parade route. Many people had small bunches of shamrock pinned to their coats. Children carried tricolors, and a few older boys had their faces painted green. He headed for the Salmon Weir Bridge, meaning to walk around the college and then circle back and maybe see the parade, maybe run into Mark and Laura. As he was waiting for the traffic to pass, he glanced down one of the side streets and saw Mark.

He was standing on the sidewalk, bareheaded, in jeans and a T-shirt, alone. Lyle had known he was thin, but there, coatless in the street, he was shockingly gaunt. As Lyle watched, Mark turned away and took two steps and stopped. He put his arms up over his face and leaned against the building, like a child counting for hide-and-seek. Farther up the street, a door opened and Laura came out. She hurried to Mark, and put her hands on his shoulders. They spoke; Lyle could see that, and that Laura's hair was in a braid, and that her dark green skirt rose and fell around her calves in the breeze, and that she was barefoot on the cold concrete. Then, slowly, she drew Mark from the wall and turned him to her. Still speaking, she took his hands and stepped backward, back toward the door she'd come out. He went with her a step, another step, and then she turned, pulling his arm around her waist, and they walked together back inside, through the door of the Salmon Weir Hostel.

The rain began again.

Lyle was glad the house was empty when he and the dog got home, empty and dim in the gray afternoon, with the glimmer of the coal fire in the sitting room. He threw away the shamrock, hung up his coat and the leash. Mark would certainly die.

He jabbed at the fire with the small poker and put some more coal on, and then he sighed and sat down in his chair and watched the fire, listened to the coal whistling as it heated. He would die. She would stand as she had there on the sidewalk this morning, and she would crumple, collapse in and down. Lyle rubbed his forehead with his fingertips.

The dog came and sat, alert, questioning, in front of him. "You're right," he said to her, "I forgot the treat. Come on." She followed him to the cupboard and gazed into his eyes as he gave her the little orange-colored biscuit.

Men would be lining up to take Mark's place, no doubt about it. The dog stayed in the kitchen to eat, as she always did, and Lyle went back to his chair. Poor bastard, knowing that. The idea of it was enough to send anybody out in shirtsleeves to grieve against the side of a building.

Then again. Maybe Laura would be one of those widows who didn't remarry. Maybe she'd dedicate herself to the children. Bring them back here in a year or two, show them where she and their father had spent these weeks. He would see her again, he thought, as the dog, her biscuit gone, trotted in; he lifted her into his lap, where she settled and fell immediately asleep. He'd see her, and she would be recovered from it.

He stroked the dog's smooth head. The wind was blowing across the chimney and making a low hooing sound; he had said before that sometimes he felt as if he were living in a jug, in this small room at the bottom of the chimney, but today he liked it. He relaxed into imagining Laura, in a few years, walking alone down by the Claddagh, and how he'd greet her, and how by then he'd have become, as he often did in dreams, younger and more attractive. Or he'd be in Idaho, somehow, and see her. At the edge of sleep, he imagined driving with her down the roads of his youth in rural Vermont, where small lanes branched off among the trees.

"Wrecked, are ye?" his wife said, and chuckled, as his heart thudded two heavy strokes.

The next day Laura looked tired, but as they met she smiled, her eyes bright, and she reached out and gripped his upper arm for an instant, and he felt again that guilty lurch of his heart. "We're going adventuring," she said, releasing his arm.

"Adventuring?" He looked at Mark, whose smile seemed tight.

Laura said, "We're going to rent a car and drive the Ring of Kerry!"

"Drive it?" Lyle said, still to Mark. "Driving's a bit of a

challenge here." Even to himself he sounded gruff, a spoil-sport.

"She'll be doing it," Mark said, and Lyle heard the injury in his voice.

"I figure, if the other tourists can manage it, so can I," she said.

"Tourists are bad drivers," Lyle said, "especially on those narrow roads."

"You've been there, then," Mark said.

"Just once," Lyle said, and told hurriedly, gruffly, about the bus tour along the narrow roads, the hordes of rude Americans and Germans.

"But the car-rental man said that wouldn't be true now, this early in the year," Laura said, her eyes strained but her voice still gay. "And it would still be worth it—everybody says Kerry's beautiful."

You are beautiful, Lyle thought, before he could stop himself, and then his mouth went dry with the fear that he'd say it, make a fool of himself, and he lumbered on to say, "Oh, it is. It's very beautiful. The landscape."

Lyle's wife took her baths at bedtime and sometimes talked to him through the half-closed door to their bedroom. Only watery sounds came from the bathroom tonight as he put on his pajamas, trying to think where that map of Kerry might have ended up. At one time, he was sure, the maps had all been in a drawer in the kitchen, but he'd looked there earlier and found playing cards and string instead. So she'd reorganized at some point, and the maps could be anywhere. He opened the closet door quietly and stared up at the stacks of shoe boxes on the top shelf. Where'd you put the maps, he could say, and she'd say, Maps—and what'd you be wanting maps for and us with no car?

The bathwater moved. "I've not seen that old dog outside Ward's shop all week," she said.

"No?" he said, to encourage her to go on, to cover the sound of the closet door closing.

"John's had that dog for years on years, he has. A number of old dogs hereabout," she said. "Just past the school those two small dogs, the white one and the terrier, they're old. Judy down Canal Road, she's an old one, Maureen Ryder's dog. Oh—I dreamt of dogs," she said.

"Dogs?" he said, though encouragement wasn't really necessary now: she always told her dreams in endless detail.

"I'd the job of feeding them—big dogs on chains in a yard. I can still see two of them, these two bulldogs. The faces on them."

When he was a boy and something was lost, a shoe, say, or a hairbrush, his mother would stand in the kitchen and say, If I was a shoe, where would I be? So now Lyle stood beside the bed and closed his eyes and thought, If I was a road map, where would I be?

"I'd found this bright blue plastic dish—half scoop, half dish, really—and I'd filled it up with dry dog food for the bulldogs." She gave a small laugh, and he heard the sound of dripping.

He bent and looked under the bed: four suitcases. If he were a road map, he might be in a suitcase, but he couldn't, certainly, get a suitcase out and open without her hearing, and he couldn't be sure the map was there, or, if it was, that it would be in the first suitcase he opened.

"Pleased with myself, I was. And then your man comes up and he says, 'That's not enough,' he says, and then he says, 'Besides, they bite.'"

He stood up again, and knew that he was an aging man, with skinny legs inside the pajama pants that were snug around his bulging stomach, unfamiliar hair in his ears and nose. He stood and heard his wife lifting herself from the bathwater, and knew that the dream she was telling would go on in her rueful voice from behind the door until she'd finished it, and that when she came out, she'd get into bed behind him, damp in a way he'd once found so erotic it nearly choked him. And maybe this would be one of the nights she'd put her moist hand on him.

"What the hell have you done with the damned road maps?" he said.

"Road maps?" she said. She pulled the bathroom door open and stood there in her worn nightgown looking at him, the ends of her short gray hair dark and stringy with wet, dripping water down the sides of her neck. "And what'd you be wanting with road maps this time of night, cursing about it?"

"I wasn't cursing," he said.

"You were. You're cursing all the time now."

"I wouldn't be cursing if the damned maps had been where they belonged."

"I'm not your housemaid," she said.

That was from an old, worn quarrel, almost a comfort, and he took up his part. "Just because I want to find things in my own goddamned house doesn't make me an ogre," he said.

"You should watch your language," she said, "and it wouldn't hurt to go to mass once in a while."

"Oh, mass! Sure—that's always the answer, isn't it? Maybe the priest could tell me where the hell you've hidden the goddamned maps." He turned away, ready for her to say it was his fault neither of the boys went to mass anymore and that Kevin would probably marry that Jewish girl, and he'd say he hoped so, better a whining Jew than a whining Catholic. While they were saying those things, he would put on his slippers and robe, she would get into bed, and he'd go downstairs and have a drink. When he came back up in half an hour, she'd be asleep.

But she didn't say that, and she didn't move toward the bed. "For your Americans, is it?" she said, so mildly that he stopped and turned to look at her. She took her robe from the hook on the door, and nodded as she pulled it on and tied the belt. "I may have them in the hall press," she said. "Will I look for them so?"

He nodded, still confused and suspicious, and he knew he should say thank you, but she was gone down the stairs, the dog trotting behind her, and then he heard her in the hall closet, and then he heard her talking to the dog. He stood beside the bed and tried to imagine what he could say to her if he went downstairs; he could imagine nothing. When he heard the television come on, he got into bed. For many years, maybe always, she had gone to bed first or they had gone to bed together, and he found the freedom of being the only body on the mattress so comfortable and novel that he fell asleep quickly.

When he woke in the morning, the first thing he knew was that he was still alone, and a quick jolt of fear made him thrust his hand onto her side of the bed. It was warm, and at the same moment he smelled the coffee and rashers, and so he was irritated with her before he was even out of bed. It was irrational, and he knew that: for thirty years he'd waked alone in bed to the smell of the breakfast she was cooking. And yet, this morning, it seemed to him she had pretended a larger absence, and the charade had forced from him a reaction that he found embarrassing.

But maybe she'd found the maps, he thought as he went down the stairs and into the kitchen. There they lay, beside his plate.

"You found them," he said.

"Was it Donegal they were wanting?" she said. "That one's gone missing."

"No—Kerry," he said.

"Grand, then—Kerry's there," she said, sounding relieved and pleased.

After breakfast, as he was putting on his coat, she said, "I thought I'd walk along with ye this morning. I'm to meet Róisín at ten at the Franciscans, and a walk will just fill the time." She was putting her coat on as she spoke, so there was nothing he could say. "Don't forget the map," she said, and he pushed it into his coat pocket and went out the door ahead of her.

"It's a grand morning," she said approvingly as they crossed the street onto the prom, and it was—nearly windless, a hint of sun. He didn't answer, and they walked on, she with her hands in her pockets, he with one hand in his pocket and the other holding the leash.

He had little hope they wouldn't meet Mark and Laura, and when he saw them at a distance, Mark sitting on a bench and Laura standing beside him, looking out toward Mutton Island, he pulled the map from his pocket, half thinking to make a quick gift of it and be gone.

His wife took a sharp breath and murmured, "He's thin."

"He's sick," Lyle snapped, and then Laura turned and saw them, and they were too close to say more.

Mark stood, with obvious effort, and smiled, and Laura smiled, and as Mark took off his hat, Lyle realized that he couldn't look at either of them, so he smiled into the air between them and said, "Good morning. This is my wife, Mary—Mark, Laura," his voice too hearty for the words.

They shook hands and said the things people say any-where—a pleasure, how do you do, hello, Lyle smiling stu-pidly, helplessly, at the hotel across the road. Then his wife said, "How do ye find Galway?" and he could feel them hes-itate and translate before Mark said, "It's a very friendly town. We'll be sorry to leave."

"But ye'll be back, then, after your trip to Kerry?"

Again a hesitation, in which Lyle heard the crying of the gulls, before Mark said, "Well—" and then Laura said, "Actually, we've been thinking about not going to Kerry, after all. Given the roads."

Lyle looked down at the dog. Laura's voice was soft but

strained. He wondered how obvious the map in his hand was, whether he could slide it back into his pocket without drawing attention.

"Ah, they're terrible, they are," his wife agreed, dismissing Kerry the Kingdom with a quick sigh as she sat on the bench. Mark sat beside her, his hat in his hand. "The thing ye might try is Aran—have ye thought of that? There's a bus from town to Rossaveal, right to the ferry over, and then on the island they've the pony traps or the little buses, and back the same day." She laughed, comfortable, eager, sitting there with her purse on her lap as if this were a visit. "Oh, the island's lovely, 'tis—it'll be gray here and the sun bright as Arizona there."

"It sounds nice," Mark said.

"Ye might think of it," she went on, and Lyle could see now her thumbs on the purse, hidden from Mark and Laura, making rapid hard circles against the leather, "and Dublin, too—have ye been to Dublin?" She looked at Laura, who shook her head. "Oh, it's not to be missed, a day in Dublin—take the train over and back, the museums and the Book of Kells—not all in a day, of course, that'd be too much for anyone, it would, but just the National Museum, say, and they've a nice little tea shop there for your lunch." She stood up as if she'd settled something, but then she went on, hardly a breath between. "No, there's Ireland to see without Kerry, there is. Even here in Galway—how much longer is your holiday?"

"Ten days?" Mark said, glancing at Laura.

"Or less," Laura said, "depending." She shrugged and drove her hands deep into her pockets. "The children," she said.

"I miss them," Mark said. His voice was quiet, and Lyle knew he was speaking to Laura. "I'd like to spend more time with them." His voice was like Mary's was when they fought about Jimmy—that softness, thinned with the threat of tears.

"Why, of course you would," Mary said. "Of course you would. But it takes a bit to change the tickets, doesn't it?" The sympathy in her voice seemed all for the difficulty of ticket changes.

"Yes," Laura said. She turned her face to the bay for a second, let the breeze push her hair back, and then she took a step closer to Mark and touched his cheek with the backs of her fingers. "It may take some doing." Mark closed his eyes for a second, and when Laura took her hand away, he put his hat back on.

So this was the end of what he'd seen on the street: Laura and Ireland had failed, and had surrendered. Mark would die, and Laura would not. They would not go together in joy to the edge of life.

"Well, then," Mary said, holding her purse over her stomach, smiling at Laura, "ye must come to tea, mustn't they, Lyle? Come to tea—let's see, could ye come today? No, wait—that won't work, will it? Maybe tomorrow?"

"That's very kind of you," Laura said.

Mark nodded to Lyle and said, "We'll meet again before then."

"Yes, of course—of course ye will, and you can tell Lyle, and we'll see about it, will we? It's grand by the fire on some of these days, it is. And ye should be in an Irish house before ye go back. It's lovely to have met ye so," she said, and shook Mark's hand again. Then she stepped in front of Lyle and put her arms around Laura and hugged her. Laura closed her eyes and for a second let her head touch Mary's.

Then they were apart, and the dog was up and ready to go, and Lyle found that he'd gotten the map back into his pocket somehow and had a hand free to shake Mark's. Then he and his wife were walking on, the dog trotting beside them, and after a few steps his wife slid her hand under his arm and his arm bent up to hold it, and so they walked on toward the Claddagh, the wind picking up at their backs.

"Coffee as well as tea, of course," she said, "since they're Americans, and tomorrow would be fine, it would, or Saturday."

"Let's make it Saturday," he said, because she was crying,

and this was a decision they could make, although he didn't believe he'd ever see Mark or Laura again.

"Such lovely people," his wife said. "Such lovely people."

Lyle knew they were, and because his wife had said it, he wanted to say to her, So are we. He wanted to say that he wasn't a young man but he wasn't dying, and that this hand on his arm was his wife's hand—that for them the end was still far off, with difficulties and complications still to come.

Instead, he pressed her wrist against his side and said, "They are, so. And it's a sad thing, it is."

4

DIGGING

So one day a farmer—his name was Seamus Sullivan, and this was in County Mayo, not far from Knock, where, when Seamus was fifteen, the Virgin had appeared—says to the wife, I'm off up the field then, and he goes off in his boots in the early afternoon with the dog at his heel and a shovel in his hand. His only idea is to be out there as far from the house as he can go without leaving his own bit of land, digging; what he wants is the heft and smell and slide of his own earth at his command. He's not bothered by the ethics of whether a man can own something like land: he owns this field and the dirt within it, and this field goes straight down to the center of the earth.

So he goes after the roots of the furze bush. It's the first edge of spring, and thin lips of yellow show here and there on the bush. This digging is hard work, starting away from the thorny bush to make sure he's beyond the spread of the roots, but it's a long day ahead and nothing else he need do, and he dedicates himself to it. He's forty-five, still strong enough to spend the whole day driving the shovel in and piling the good dirt out, but the furze is a shallow weed. After only an hour the excuse work is mostly done, the thorny bush as root-exposed as if he were planting it instead of casting it out. So he pulls it out to the center of the field and sets it afire. Then he goes back, to crouch beside his dug pit and roll a cigarette with his dog lolling beside him while the bush burns. It's a pitch-filled thing, a furze bush, and so it burns hot and fast; as he tosses the damp end bit of tobacco and paper away, he sees the wife standing down by the house shading her eyes to watch the last of the flames. Bridget, just a girl still after two years of being married to him, who's older than her husband ought to be. That's enough: he stands and takes up his shovel again.

Maybe the sun comes out for a few minutes, and it feels so good to be digging in the thin sunlight in his field that he wonders why he doesn't do this once a week, his muscles limber, the rhythm steady, and then his shovel hits something not dirt. Even that, even the challenge of going now into the next layer of his land, where rocks will complicate the digging, even that feels good. He moves the shovel back a few inches and drives it in again and lifts up the dirt and sees there, mud-encrusted and bent, a chalice, the gold pale and shining where his shovel has struck it.

So there stands Seamus, rubbing the dirt from the cup with his broad callused fingers for a few seconds before he looks guiltily down the slope to see if Bridget is still watching him. She isn't, so he has a chance to decide—will he keep digging and see if there's more? Will he take just this one thing? Will he have a good look and then, tenderly, tuck it back where it came from and put back the dirt and pray for the grass to grow over it all?

In this same midafternoon, in Cork instead of Mayo, Mary Alice O'Driscoll comes hurrying along the road into Clonakilty, tears in her pretty eyes. She's nineteen and a strapping girl, tall and strong, and she has dreams. This is a difficult situation, being a strapping girl with dreams, because nobody believes the combination is natural. Her sister, Rosie, is the beauty, and people assume she has dreams, but Mary Alice is sturdy, and her mother, a practical woman, sees no reason for Mary Alice not to marry Jimmy Curtin, who owns his own boat and has the hope of a house when his father passes on. He's a hard worker and a decent man, and if Mary Alice would just be reasonable, she'd see that decency is quite a bit to get in a husband, and Jimmy's not that old, not forty yet, and he fancies the girl.

Mary Alice is reasonable, so she's already abandoned any number of dreams without ever having mentioned them to anyone—gracefulness, for example, and a piano, and a quick wit in conversation, a holiday in Switzerland, and a wedding in St. Colman's Cathedral in Queenstown, the most beautiful thing she's ever seen and as far from Rosscarbery as she's ever been—but now her mother says she can't go to the dance on Saturday in Glandore. It shouldn't matter, after all those other things she knows she'll never have, but it does matter. Mary Alice believes her heart is breaking. So she's on her way down the road to complain to her Aunt Margaret, who was the strapping sister herself and knows where you end up if you don't hold on to some dream— where she is, housekeeper to the priest.

So here's Mary Alice, her head up so the tears won't spill, tapping at the kitchen door of the priest's house, tapping and tapping, and it isn't until Father Moran himself, a book in his hand, pulls open the door that she realizes that she's come away into town with her apron still on and her hair still in last night's plait. Not that Father Moran is tidy either, standing there in his stocking feet and his hair mussed as if he's just waked up and here it is almost time for his tea. Oh Father, she says, I'm sorry to bother you, I was looking for Aunt Margaret. You were of course, he says, but because he has, indeed, only just waked from a doze in his chair, his voice is much curter than he'd intended, and Mary Alice loses her hold on her tears, and they fall from her pretty eyes in two silver lines down her face.

She has no idea how lovely she looks to Father Moran, who isn't a young man but isn't old enough to be her father, either.

Father Moran himself hardly has an idea of how lovely she looks to him, at this dusky moment in the kitchen when her Aunt Margaret isn't there and he's barely awake and can't tell exactly who he is, priest or man, but he manages to say, Here now, what's this all about.

Mary Alice can't say what it's all about, not to him, not in his stocking feet, and so she sobs four times trying to think of an appropriate thing to say to a priest, and says, I was thinking of St. Colman's Cathedral.

Father Moran has seen St. Colman's Cathedral, so he almost understands why this girl—he's known her name at some moment, though it escapes him now—weeps so hopelessly, and he's touched by it, and moved to transfer his book from his left hand to his right, and to reach his left hand out to touch and comfort her. He means to pat his hand against her shoulder in a fatherly, priestly gesture, but his hand takes itself instead to her cheek, where the tears are cool against her firm, warm skin.

As soon as she spoke, Mary Alice began to actually think of St. Colman's, its soaring beauty, and how she'll never be a bride there, never have a life that includes a piano or quick wit or holidays, all because her mother won't allow her to go to the dance in Glandore this Saturday night, where some young man might magically appear who would love her, and when the priest's gentle hand touches her tears, she has no choice in the matter: she covers his hand with her own and presses it to her face, and before either of them is quite certain how or why such a thing could happen, his book is on the floor and their mouths are sweet together with salt tears on all their lips.

By now, Seamus has come in for his tea, with his chest full of his secret. Bridget sees that he's got something going on, something that makes him feel big this evening, and she wonders about it as she cuts the bread. He's been nowhere, just up the field the whole day, digging. She has her doubts about whether potatoes will grow there in the second field, the sun's so poor below the hill, but it's not hers to say. What is hers is this house, this empty house, with no child in it.

Come up, he says behind her, and she hears the dog clip from her corner and into his lap.

So, Bridget thinks. So. And she cuts the bread thicker; when she's done, she cooks him a buttered egg and brings out the last jar of her sister's blackberry jam as well. Her sister has the five boys and two girls. Is it Christmas, he says when he comes to the table, but he's gentle about it, and she smiles just a bit, pouring the tea. The field's ready, is it, she says, and he says it is, nearly.

After the meal he goes out with the dog and smokes again, looking up at the field where the cup and four golden bracelets lie hidden in the dirt, though he can feel their presence still behind his ribs. He's dug them a deeper hiding place up there, and will leave it all for now. He's nowhere to sell it, and no idea how to explain where he's gotten the money if he did. Besides, he thinks the gold isn't that kind of treasure. It's something else, and he's spent the afternoon trying to get it figured out—how the gold stands for something ancient and splendid and connected to him—and he's decided that, when he's got it straight in his head, the time will come, and he'll go to the priest and tell him what he's found, and ask him to write to the proper people so they can come and get it and take it to the museum. They'll make a card for it, he thinks, saying Seamus Sullivan, County Mayo. The idea of that card has been growing in him all day, a weighted restlessness in his chest, as he's been digging. He'll plant potatoes there, when it's time, and the time will come. It's no sin, he's sure, to take his pleasure privately now, in thinking of himself as a man with gold in his field. No sin either to turn to his wife in bed tonight and take that pleasure as well, and when the time comes, when the washing-up is done and the fire's banked and the two of them sigh into their rest, he does so, and she answers to him gladly, a rare easy sweetness between them. Falling asleep, his last thought is of the shimmering power of gold hidden in a field; hers is that this may get them a child.

Before that happens, back in the kitchen in Clonakilty, Mary Alice, weak in the knees, and Father Moran, utterly without a thought in his head, linger through the long moment of their kiss, as if dependent for balance on their joined mouths, as if suspended from each other's lips, or from their hands on her cheek. And then, of course, there's a sound from somewhere, the necessary reminder that Aunt Margaret hasn't vanished from the earth, that priests and girls with pretty eyes aren't free to kiss in kitchens in this world, and they lurch apart. For a single second they stare at one another, blankly, and then the horror gathers. She turns and flies out of the house and down the narrow street of the town, eyes dry now and nearly blind. As soon as she's free of the houses, she turns off the road and sets out across the fields for home.

A mile or so along, as she's walking more slowly but still not daring to think of anything, she sees below her the ring of standing stones people call the Druid's Altar. The light is failing fast, and the stones take on the look of giant, shawled women, some standing, some kneeling, and she takes herself down from the little ridge to them, between them, into the center of the circle.

I've kissed a priest, she says aloud.

Maybe she sways, with the enormity of what she's done, and it's just an illusion that the stone women stir, but Mary Alice O'Driscoll takes to her heels again, not waiting to see whether the druid's women are welcoming her or casting her out. She takes to her heels, down across the fields in the twilight now, and she rushes in to her mother in the kitchen getting the tea with a scowl on her face and, breathless, she says, I'll marry him, Mother—I'll marry Jimmy if you say. What else could she do, a girl who'd tempt a priest and bring stones to life confessing it? If she didn't marry as quick as that, who knows what shame she might bring on them all?

So say this was a Tuesday, in March, in 1910. By Sunday, when the banns are read for Mary Alice O'Driscoll and James Patrick Curtin, Seamus Sullivan has been laid to rest (that weight in his chest his heart failing, and he never knew, dreaming of his neighbors thumping his back in congratulation when the gold came pouring out of his land, and he may be dreaming it still, if heaven is as it should be), and Bridget's brother, Pat, has walked the three fields and found them poor, Seamus's plan for potatoes in the second field foolishness. He'll let it go back to grass and put his own sheep on it. He does that, and takes Bridget to keep his house for him half a mile away, and when her son is born in the winter, Pat will be the one who insists he be named Kevin, for their father, instead of Seamus for his own. And by that time, down in Cork, Mary Alice will be amazed to discover herself a little in love with Jimmy Curtin, whose awkward chatter covers a thousand apt generosities, and when their first child is born the next year, there's no question of his name at all, it's James. There's no question either, when the chance comes for them (three more of them now, all strapping children), through the death of a cousin and the emigration of three others, to move to a small house in Galway, and no question that the boys will follow their father as fishermen. In fact, the only question that ever arises that disturbs Mary Alice is when her James comes to her at the age of fifteen and says, Mother, I've a calling to be a priest. You have not, she says, but he scowls, says, Why not? I've the marks, and Father Kennedy says—and what can she say but, I don't care what Father Kennedy says, you'll be no priest? That's as close as she'll ever come to allowing herself to remember the forbidden salty kiss in the kitchen, and that's a story she'll never tell to a soul.

Seamus's story of finding the gold never gets told either, and the gold never found, so when Bridget dies with Kevin only eleven, his Uncle Pat sees no reason not to take him off to America, where things'll have to be better than they are at home with all the mess there is now—it's 1921, and who knows how things will turn out? So off they go, leaving the two houses to fall down around themselves, and if South Boston doesn't vault Pat into the prosperity he'd expected, it does vault young Kevin into a world of street corners and movies and, once he leaves school when he's just fifteen, pubs and nicknames and fistfights. He's one of a gang of fellows on the corner of E. Street and Bowen; they all live at home and work here and there on the docks and in the factories, fight about anything, spend their money foolishly, and try to impress the girls. When Kevin's twenty, he falls mad in love with a girl five years older, and before he knows what he's about, he's going to be a father. It's 1931 now, and there's nothing to be done but take his bride back to the cramped flat over the barbershop and Uncle Pat's vicious hospitality. He's twenty-one when his son, Lyle, is born, and twenty-two on Christmas Eve, far gone in drink, when he decides to swim the icy Charles River to sober up before going home to the wife and kid.

This same Christmas Eve, 1932, back in Galway City, James Curtin, who has put away his wish to be a priest as his mother once put away her wish to go to Switzerland, proposes marriage to Norah Silke, who turns him down, and two months later he marries her sister, Maeve. They have a daughter, Róisín, and then another daughter, Mary, and then sons; before the sons are old enough to go out on the boat, which James has always hated, he sells the boat and buys a poor bit of land, but he's no talent as a farmer, and when his children offer to leave—Mary to America, one son to be a priest, another to Australia—he's glad to have them go. He's a harsh man and real poverty makes him more so, but he's no worse than other fathers, better than some, which Maeve tells the children so often even she believes it.

So when Lyle Sullivan and Mary Curtin meet at last, in 1960 at a huge company picnic on Cape Cod, they could have a load of stories to tell one another, but they don't. Mary doesn't work for the company, but she's come with a girlfriend who does, and the girlfriend insists that Mary's perfectly welcome. Her whole life—she's twenty-four— Mary has worried about being where she doesn't belong, and she's never quite figured out where she does belong. When she knew she was to come to America, she was terrified and excited; once she got here, she was so homesick she'd have gone back if there'd been the money, and if the ones at home hadn't needed the money she sent. She can't imagine living her whole life so far from home, but she can't imagine, quite, anymore, now that she's been here a year, what life she'd be living if she were still there. So even here, at a picnic, she doesn't dare go very far from her friend but doesn't quite join in any conversations either. That's where she is when Lyle first sees her, just a little outside.

He doesn't know that she looks a lot like his grandmother Bridget, who wore her long, dark, curling hair much the way Mary's got hers, in a soft bun high on her head, and whose mouth had a similar sweet patience. He doesn't know what Bridget looked like because he's never seen the one photograph of her, which his mother hoards, along with the eight other things that belonged to his father, Kevin, in a locked metal box in the back of her closet. He won't even find that box until after his mother's dead in three years; when Mary comes back from Ireland to marry him then, she'll have cut her hair and taken to setting it on brush rollers for the bouffant effect that's the American style in 1963. So this day, on Cape Cod, all he knows is that she looks good to him. He doesn't even think of her as pretty, although she is, and it's a good thing he doesn't: he long ago developed the unconscious habit of avoiding anything that might distract him from his duty to his mother, and so he never speaks to girls he thinks of as pretty. This isn't exactly his mother's fault: she's not exactly old in her mid-fifties, not exactly bitter or pitiful. True, she's always tried to impress upon Lyle the dangers of drink and wild friends, but hasn't she good reason for that, since drink and wild friends killed her young husband and left her with this son to raise and no skills beyond laundry work, that she couldn't do anymore after she hurt her back that time when Lyle was only seventeen? Not exactly her fault, or his, but it's come to this, that Lyle lives the life of a middle-aged husband, although he's only twenty-eight. He's good at his office job with the hardware company, frugal, responsible. He likes some television programs, and he likes to drink a beer or, more rarely, a little whiskey and play a game or two of hearts in the evening with his mother in the oddly comforting cloud of her cigarette smoke. He's not unhappy, and he's not particularly eager to marry, but still, this pretty day on Cape Cod, the girl in the dark skirt and soft blouse looks good to him, and he keeps an eye on her, the way she's shy but cheery, and when he passes almost accidentally near enough to hear her talking with her friend, he hears that she's Irish, and he's a goner.

He doesn't recognize that he's a goner, though. He's never been a goner before. As a teenager back in Vermont, he kissed a few girls, longed in a shameful way for others, and once since he brought his mother back to Boston to live, he dated one woman three times, but he's never been a goner. He thinks he feels sorry for this girl, so far from home, and that in itself is so unusual for him that it's almost dusk, almost time for the fireworks, before he finds a way to meet her.

She's alone at last—her friend has gone to find them some more lemonade. Mary's alone, crouching to spread the blanket where she and her friend will sit to watch the fireworks, and it's coming on dusk, and the ocean is stirring, and she hasn't the least hint how appealing she looks to Lyle. He sees the domesticity of her task, and remembers the quick dancing foreign murmur of her voice. He isn't given to imagining (Mary's friend works in his department, calls him rude and bossy), but he imagines she might be lonely, and that's what he means to ask her when he comes up beside her—he means to say something like, You're far from home, in the sort of joking tone he assumes men use with women they haven't met yet. Instead he says, Hello—I'm Lyle Sullivan from Production Control, just as if it were a staff meeting, and Mary gives a little leap, she's so startled.

She hasn't been thinking of home, exactly, but of underwear, actually, her own, specifically, and, generally, the difference between Irish underwear and American underwear in her own admittedly limited experience. Her job is minding the children of the Cunninghams in Brookline, who loaned her the fare to come over. The oldest of them is a girl, twelve, a rather pretty girl, who has been teasing her mother for pettipants; for days now Mary's been wondering in odd moments just what pettipants might be, whether it's something she ought to buy. In April she finished paying her debt to the Cunninghams, and she sends half her small salary back to Róisín each month and saves most of the rest, but she has a bit she keeps out for pleasure, and she's wondering if the cost of pettipants (which she doesn't know) would match the pleasure of them. That's what she's wondering when this fellow comes up and startles her.

She blushes because of the underwear, and because he's the fellow she'd noticed earlier and asked her friend about, and because, as she knew someone would, he has recognized that she has no right to be at the picnic.

He blushes because he hadn't meant to startle her, and hadn't meant to say such a stupid thing, but there they are.

Mary straightens up and puts out her hand. I'm Mary Curtin from Galway, she says, and she smiles because she's relieved at last of the dread of discovery that's tagged behind her all day. I don't work for the company, she says.

He's handsomer than she'd thought, though she'd thought him handsome enough in the sunshine and from a distance.

She's lovely, looking up at him and that smile, the quick cooing way she says doon't and coompany, and he nearly forgets to shake her hand.

Maybe the first of the rockets goes up then and bursts in gold and silver in the sky that becomes, that suddenly, the perfect darkness, or maybe Lyle gathers his wits and asks where Galway is, or where she does work, and they talk a little more before her friend comes back and Lyle takes his leave. They won't turn out to be the sort of couple that reminisces about their first meeting; years from now, when their younger son, Jimmy, asks her, bitterly, How did you end up with him anyway? she'll just say, I met him at a picnic. If in saying that she remembers any of this—the fireworks, and how the crowd around her made a full reverent chorus of their pleasure while she hugged to herself the thrilling certainty that shy, handsome Lyle Sullivan from Production Control fancied her—she won't say so.

It'll be their older son, Kevin, when he's about ten and just curious, who asks his father, Did Mom used to be pretty? Maybe the question lurches Lyle back to this moment, standing in the dark beneath the brilliant, slow explosions of light, studying how straight her back is, and she turns and bends toward her friend and something in the tilting of her body wallops him with a desire so harsh he makes a sound. Maybe that's why his answer to his son is so harsh—What difference does that make?—but he couldn't tell his son that, could he? Or how he was utterly certain, talking to her, that if he put out his hand and touched the spun darkness of the hair at her temple, her smile would only deepen?

So. No stories get told this night on Cape Cod, and the story of this night will never be told, even between them, but it goes on for all that—Lyle goes home a goner, Mary goes home just as bad, and then the waiting part begins, because this is still 1960, long before young ladies began telephoning young men, and this is still Lyle, who hasn't stopped being cautious and mostly content just because of the way a girl he met says, It's grand, so, and makes him imagine touching her hair. When he can't quite get her voice out of his head but begins to be afraid that he doesn't remember it quite right, he still has to work his way around to finding out where she is, and that involves her friend in his department, and with one thing and another it's well into September before he telephones her and asks her to a movie. She says yes, and says yes when he calls her again although it's October by then; this is the pattern of almost involuntary patience she'll never quite lose, and he'll never quite recognize as patience, which will make him even more impatient with everyone else in his life, including his sons, who won't practice it on his behalf. But by the time he calls her again, to invite her to Thanksgiving dinner to meet his mother (things have gone that well already, or that inevitably), she's gone.

Years later, she'll tell stories of her childhood, of Irish people and Irish adventures, funny stories and inspiring stories and now and then a sad story, but she'll never tell the story of how she answers the doorbell and takes the telegram that is addressed to Mary Curtin and stares at it as if it weren't her own name. She'll never explain how distant her own horror at herself seems when she reads the words MOTHER DYING and hears herself thinking, I'd be too late. She'll never admit that she doesn't know what she'd have done next if her employer hadn't come into the corridor then and asked what was wrong.

But she doesn't have to know that, because Mrs. Cunningham does come into the corridor, and so Mary does the right things. She explains, she apologizes: she has the price of the ticket back in her savings, she must go, she doesn't know if she'll come back. She does it all with dignity and calm, the telephoning, the packing, the leaving itself, and it isn't until she's on the plane and night has fallen that the terrible thick guilt of it begins to squeeze her across the chest.

She lands in Shannon, takes the Galway bus, and gets out in the still-early morning in Oranmore. A man happens to come up the footpath and sees her, and says, You'd be the Curtin girl come back from America, and when she says, Yes, he says, Sorry for your trouble, so she knows, as she walks the last three miles, that she's too late, and she doesn't need the black ribbon on the door of the house to choke her with grief and regret, and she doesn't need Róisín's bitterness to make her feel the tug of the halter of shame at the nape of her neck, but she gets it anyway.

Róisín opens the door to her and turns back into the house without a word. It's left to Mrs. Carey, who's come to help, to ask, Would you see her, and so Mary steps unwelcomed and unembraced into the front room still in her coat and touches her mother's hand for the last time. She knows what her mother would say, what a load Róisín has carried alone this last year. As she stands there in the cold, Mary accepts Róisín's bitterness as just, and bearable. She believes that before spring she'll be back in America; if the Cunninghams don't want to sponsor her again, Father Martin may find her someone else. Or she can get some kind of work here and save.

But when she comes out of that room, meaning to put her suitcase in a corner and take up some task in preparation for the wake, her father has come in the house, and Róisín dries her hands to come and embrace her. I was taken strange, Róisín says, seeing you there so American in your coat. You're welcome, Mary, she says, you're welcome home again. The tea is on, she says.

Mary's mortally tired, thirty hours since she slept. She kisses her sister and turns to kiss her father, who stands beside the fire. It's good you've come, he says, with Róisín off in Galway City now.

Off? Mary says.

Oh, Róisín says, with the breath of a laugh, I didn't write it to you but Michael Carey and I are being married, she says. In Christmas week.

Mary stares, Róisín grins, Da folds his arms and snorts. Did you think you were away? he says.

For just that one moment, Mary believes they have killed her, but in the next moment she is simply lost, unhappy, and at home.

Right then, without a cup of tea or a bit of rest, she accepts their tribal, intimate revenge, begins her penance for the sins of abandonment, hope, desire.

She takes on her mother's work and then her sister's, and protects her heart with prayer and exhaustion. She doesn't recognize the slow creep of hopelessness, doesn't know she's sinking, settling into the suffocating bog of it, until Lyle's letter arrives in mid-January and she finds herself unable to breathe.

It's only a letter, and rather short, though she reads it a dozen times. He writes about the weather, which is bad in Boston this winter, and says he's being promoted at work. He doesn't mention that his mother's had a stroke and he spends his evenings now, after the nurse has gone, trying to pretend she isn't drooling, trying to pretend he doesn't understand her demands for cigarettes he'll have to hold for her. He never does tell Mary about that first year, or the guilt that stains his relief when he finally puts his mother into a nursing home and lives alone but still not free of her in the apartment they shared for so long. In the same way, Mary never tells him about Da's growing strangeness—the way he's taken to shouting up the chimney and hiding food and sometimes staring at her as if he suspects her of something—or Róisín's small, breezy cruelties. She writes instead of the weather and farming in Oranmore; he tells her about Irish politics, and she tells him droll bits about Irish people; she wonders about movies and he tells her she's not missing much. After the first year, she asks him about world affairs and he mentions his mother's illness; he writes vaguely of hoping to travel and she mentions her sister's babies and her youngest brother's departure for work in England; she asks about his work and he explains why it's only sensible to buy a house rather than rent. It's an odd and awkward courtship, but it sustains their hearts through a long dark time.

And then one day in the third year, a week to the day after his mother's death, Lyle drives to a travel agency. His only idea is to be going somewhere, away from the empty apartment and the closet full of his mother's things, to be making arrangements, putting large and permanent things in motion and order. He writes a check; in four days he'll be on the airplane for Dublin, where he'll get a train to Galway and a bus to Oranmore. He figures he can take a taxi from there, or rent a bicycle, or walk, if he has to. He isn't bothered by the propriety of paying an unannounced transatlantic call on a woman he's met only three times: he wants to see her, and she's always said yes, and he has nowhere else to go.

At the same moment—though it's late afternoon there on the small farm in County Galway—Mary is sitting on her bed dabbing a wet rag on the cut on her cheekbone Da's punch opened. She's panting, but not as badly as she was, and although she keeps a wary eye on her door, she isn't really afraid. Still, something will have to be done: she'll clean herself up and walk to Galway and talk with Róisín. She can't talk him past these sudden rages anymore, and with nobody left at home except her, it's only a matter of time and opportunity before he knocks down somebody who doesn't love him.

Five days later, as the two elderly gardai lean smoking against their car with her suddenly cooperative father, Mary searches under his bed for the shoes he says he's got to have if he's to go with the lads to St. Bridget's Hospital. She finds a plate of moldy potatoes, two copies of *Key of Heaven,* three knives, and a sock stuffed full of one- and five-pound notes. And the shoes. She runs to the car with the shoes, her heart pounding, and she says, Da, and he meets her eyes with his sly ones, and winks. For an instant there in the thin sunshine, he's the father of her best childhood mornings. Your mother made me them stockings, he says. Did she, she says. She did, he says, yawning, fine heavy stockings. I'm off so, he says, and throws the cigarette away.

She watches the car down the yard, and she's crying, of course, but she'd hardly be human if some corner of her heart weren't preparing to wake into something new, if some corner of her mind weren't calculating how much money a sock could hold. So when she imagines that the fellow wobbling along the road now on a bicycle looks like Lyle Sullivan, she tells herself, I'd not be human if I didn't think of him now, but in penance for that humanity, she stands a minute longer, waiting for him to pass by and prove her foolishness.

5

PENUMBRA

Mark and Laura had come to Ireland, though neither of them had said so, in pursuit of a miracle caused by joy. In the months between his diagnosis and their trip, Mark had believed in his death only for brief moments, shudders of a fear that was near euphoria and that gave way almost immediately to shy pride, as if he'd discovered that he had a talent previously unsuspected by anyone. It was true: he, Mark Driscoll, high-school history teacher, husband, father, as ordinary a person as he could imagine, had an incurable fatal disease, and was dying. It seemed impossible that he should be doing something so outrageously dramatic. Who am I to be doing such a thing? he'd nearly think. The cancer itself was real, of course—the treatments, the discomfort and expense and awkwardness of it. He'd lost his hair; his face was swollen by medication; he'd grown terribly thin; his balance had become poor; he had no desire for food or sex;

even sleep was rarely restful. He knew that strangers found him grotesque and that old friends pitied him, and pitied Laura because she was burdened with him. He pitied her too. So when she proposed the trip to Ireland, he agreed: maybe something would happen. A miracle seemed to him no more unlikely, no more inexplicable, than dying. In any case, they'd always wanted to go to Ireland.

And then, without warning, halfway through their three-week stay, on St. Patrick's Day, as they were dressing to go out for a walk, a moment of terror came and stayed, deepened, thickened: he was suddenly blind with it, and staggered wild out of the room in the hostel where Laura stood barefoot braiding her hair, careened down the short hall and into the street. He knew it, knew it: he was going to be dead. Five more months, maybe six, the oncologist had said in February, and he'd thought then, Oh, that's good, it'll all be over well before the holidays. But now, for the first time, he knew that he would be dead, and he could not bear it, and he stood in the chilly Galway street and wept in helpless, wordless fear against the side of a building.

Laura came and got him, and helped him back inside, to the room, to the bed, and sat with him, her hand on his chest, until the sobbing stopped and he was quiet.

When he could speak, he said, "I'm afraid."

"Of course you are," she said. "So am I," and then, quietly, sadly, she began telling her fears—the loneliness, the children's confusion, the future without his company, growing old and facing her own death without him.

She had said these things before; maybe the story of her widowhood comforted her. But hearing her tell it, he realized now, had pleased him. He'd been flattered, he could see now, and the tawdriness of that, its near obscenity, forced a groan from his chest, and he turned his face to the wall.

"Listen," she said, "it's been raining for two days, and we've been stuck in here. That's all this is—bad cabin fever." She patted his back briskly. "What we need to do is get out, go somewhere. I think we should rent a car and go to Kerry."

He couldn't say his fear, how absolute it had been, and he couldn't say what this was, now, this deep shadow of that fear, this understanding that life had nothing to do with him. Nothing mattered. Nothing at all. "All right," he murmured, and for the rest of that day and the next, he did as she suggested—dressing, eating, walking within the flurry of her telephone calls and guidebook consultations, her plans for this complicated excursion to Kerry, the Ring of Kerry, Kerry the Kingdom. The darkness weighted his bones, his tongue, his vision, his mind: he would be dead. No: he would *be* nothing. He would not *be*. He felt only and obscurely that he should behave well, cause no pain or trouble.

He slept thinking that and woke the second morning beside her. He could feel that she was awake, lying quiet at the slight distance they kept between them now, since sex had stopped—the distance that had once held the pettiness and comfortable meannesses and easy generosities of marriage but was now filled with careful politeness. He was chilly, and thought of the blanket on their bed at home: it was a wool blanket; it had been pretty expensive; they had discussed buying it; it was a blanket like the blankets of his childhood, weighty and rough.

He wanted it. To be there, under that blanket, in the bed and room and house that had been his for so long, was a thing he wanted, and he said aloud, "Laura, we have to go home, now, today."

She stroked his back. "You know we can't do that," she said.

"Jesus," he said, "why not?"

She stopped her hand and then took it away. In his mind he imagined her answers to his question: the cost of changing tickets, Kerry, he'd feel better soon—and to all the answers he replied silently, So what, so what?

"You're upset," she said, gently.

"I'm not upset, Laura—I'm dying, and I want to do it at home, not on the damned sidewalk in a foreign country."

He knew now that he would not die heroically, or with wisdom or humor, or by the generous courage of suicide; he wished, at least, to do it privately. He insisted, bluntly, immovably, as they dressed and ate and walked beside the bay and came back to the hostel, and there, hours later, finally, she agreed.

And then, as she left the room to begin the necessary telephone calls, an island, distant and stone blue, surfaced through the calmed despair of his mind.

All through the afternoon, while he dozed and Laura talked to travel agents and to family back in Idaho, the small island grew more solid, soothing him, even when she reported that they couldn't get a flight with connections until Thursday. As evening fell and she finished, and came and sat on the edge of the bed beside him and sighed, it had come so close and real that he could almost make out the welter of stone walls, the noise of waves against cliffs.

"We've still got three days," she said into the near dark. "Maybe we could do something."

"Two full days," he agreed. "Not long enough to get to Kerry and back, is it?" he said, barely a question.

"No," she said softly, and then, "but thanks," and in a moment she went on. "Maybe we could go to the Aran Islands—Lyle's wife said it would be sunny there." She had her hands in fists in her lap, tapping her knuckles together.

Lyle was an older American man they'd met and chatted with most mornings on their walk beside the bay—a man, Mark had thought before, pretty obviously smitten with Laura, and embarrassed by it, because he was quite a bit older, and because Mark was sick, a poor rival. Mark had found it a little irritating that Laura had been so oblivious, but he hadn't quite been willing to tease her about it. And then this morning Lyle's wife had come with him, so maybe she'd noticed it, too, in something Lyle had said, or hadn't said. At any rate, she'd come along this morning, and she had said the Aran Islands were sunny—"Bright as Arizona," in fact—and he'd forgotten, had hardly heard her, but surely that suggestion explained this island in his mind.

"When we get home it'll still be March," Laura said, hurrying through something wretched in her voice. "We could use a little sun."

She had given up a great deal, so he asked, "Is that what you want?" and when she said, "Yes," he said, "All right, then—tomorrow?"

"I think the bus for the ferry leaves at nine and three." She reached across his chest and turned on the lamp. "I'll get the tour book. Maybe we could take the later one, and spend the night?"

The light and the book, with its photographs and advice, replaced the odd bare island of his imagination with Inishmore, the largest of the three islands, where they'd see the huge ring fort and hidden holy wells, and buy sweaters for the children. He didn't mind: when this was over, they would go home, where he would wait, among familiar faces and familiar things, to die.

The ferry was a good-size boat, with an open deck on top and another at the rear, and a big windowed cabin below. Mark and Laura sat there, inside, protected from the wind and spray and excitement of actually being on the sea. "You can sit outside if you want to," he said, and she said no, she was all right. She might nap a bit, she said, and he might want to, too. He agreed, and the steady rhythm of the ferry's engine sent him to the edge of sleep; the island met him there again, rising beyond a stretch of jumbled boulders where huge glistening seals, their backs mottled gray and brown, gazed steadily past him, wise and placid, out to sea.

When he awoke, the ferry was slowing, and he knew they were approaching the real island. They waited, as had become their pattern, for most of the others to leave; then they made their slow way up the steps and across the little gangplank onto the pier at Kilronan, Inishmore.

The wind was cold, but the sun shone brilliantly, on five minibuses lining the pier and, farther up, a dozen or so pony traps standing beside the road that led around a small beach. A ruddy-faced Irish man in a tweed Irish cap stood by each bus and each two-wheeled cart, calling out his offer of a tour to the people leaving the ferry. Beyond, on the slope behind a very tall, clearly modern Celtic cross, crowded the buildings that must be the village proper: a hotel, two pubs, other low buildings he couldn't identify.

All of it struck Mark as shabby, after the clean, wild barrenness of the island in his mind, but Laura said, "Oh, isn't it pretty?" so he kept that thought to himself. He said, "Well, here we are—what'll we do?"

"We ought to take one of those pony carts," she said, and her face was bright. "The book says they take you halfway up the island, to that big stone fort."

They walked slowly, and Mark watched a couple get into one of the carts, and then watched them grab the sides, their faces startled, as the pony began trotting and they bounced away. He shook his head. "I don't think my unpadded bones would take it," he said. "Why don't we find a place to sit down and take a look at the guidebook—see what's nearby."

She shrugged, and he could feel her disappointment, but she said, "Okay—how about over there," pointing. There, at the lowest edge of the village, in front of a pair of new-looking sweater shops, a low wall curved behind several concrete benches.

As they walked past the pony carts and then around the small beach, among the other tourists and around the groups hurrying to board the return ferry, Mark hoped there'd be something to see, something pleasant for her and possible for him.

"All right?" she said, and her voice was so simply kind he

was ashamed: she was kind, and this was the last of the Irish adventures—he should try to make it pleasant for her, at least. He thought of saying that Lyle's wife had been right about the sun, and then he thought he'd do better than that—he'd tell her that Lyle thought she was beautiful, and without thinking further, he said, "Lyle was attracted to you, you know."

"Lyle?" she said. "Oh—Lyle."

"He was. That's why he was so awkward when his wife came along."

She laughed softly and shook her head. They came to the benches and sat down.

"No, really," Mark said. "I'm serious."

"Oh, don't be silly," she said. She squeezed his hand and let it go, and opened her bag to find the guidebook.

"He probably dreams about you."

"I doubt that," she said, but he could see color rising in her cheek. She opened the book to the index in the back.

Her dismissal of his compliment made him stubborn. "Well, I know what I'm talking about," he said. "I've wanted some women that way." A gull glided in and began foraging in front of them. "You remember Kathy—she lived across from us in married student housing? I used to think about her all the time, that long hair of hers. And then when I first started teaching at Polk High, there was a science teacher, Joanna. I don't know if you ever even met her, but there was something about her hands." He watched the gull, thinking distantly of how much it looked like a pigeon, really. "Sometimes I'd be driving home, and the way she moved her hands would leap into my mind and take my breath away." Across the little bay, return passengers were filing onto the ferry. "And then Toni—remember Toni?" He turned to her then, and saw that she did, and he saw, too, that she was waiting to be injured, but he found he couldn't stop. "I didn't actually dream about her, but I used to wake up Sundays sometimes, thinking about what it would be like—"

"For heaven's sake, Mark," she said, and that did stop him.

"I never did anything," he said.

Her eyes didn't change.

"I didn't," he said, and he heard the resentment in his own voice, and he was astonished at it. What had he expected? He had meant to pay her a compliment, at first, and then he'd begun bullying her with his memories—had he thought she'd be grateful?

And yet, behind all that, his resentment was real. He had tried to be nice, to be pleasant, to assure her of her attractiveness, and here she was with this accusing stare, as if he'd confessed infidelity. He'd been faithful, if faithful meant he'd never said anything, never touched another woman in other than a publicly affectionate way. But he had loved those women, in a way, and half a dozen others, desiring them through long afternoons and upon waking and while driving home. "I just found them attractive," he said.

Slowly, her eyes hard now, she nodded, and turned from him to look out over the water, her hands tight on the book in her lap.

"I don't anymore," he said. "I don't feel that way anymore. About anybody."

She nodded again, without looking at him. "I know," she said. "It's all right."

"I just thought you should know," he said.

"It's all right," she said again, and carefully put the book back in her bag. She stood up. "I'm going to find a B&B." She adjusted the red scarf she wore over the shoulders of her coat, but she didn't look at him.

"Shall I wait here?" he said.

"That's a good idea," she said, and turned and walked away, toward the big cross and the clutter of village beyond it.

He watched her, seeing as if it were new how jaunty her walk was when she was angry. And she was certainly angry, and probably had a right to be.

They'd talked about confessions in the support group he'd attended until Christmas, solemnly justifying their desire to set every record straight. And then one guy, even younger than Mark, had said, "Okay—so you tell it all, right? And then they say, 'Hey, you're in remission.' And then they say, 'Hey, you're cured!' And then she says, 'You bastard—you're history.' " Secretly willing to jinx marriage if that could bring a cure, giddy with the possibility, they'd laughed almost to tears.

He had managed not to confess that he'd never really liked the couch she'd chosen, that he hadn't actually applied for the promotion he hadn't gotten, that he wouldn't have chosen to have a third child, even that he actually preferred his beef well done. And now, after all that, out of the dozens of misunderstandings that must now, in kindness, be allowed to stand—after all that, and knowing better (he could admit it now, alone on the bench), he'd gone and blundered into the worst of them.

She disappeared up the road into the village, and he turned back to the water. He was right about Lyle—he'd seen Lyle's face when Laura touched his arm as she spoke, seen how he watched her touch her own hair. Laura was beautiful as well as good. And yet, even before he got sick, he hadn't longed for her in years, not in that nearly swooning way Lyle's eyes had betrayed. Not in the way he had longed for other women. That was still true, even if he shouldn't have said any of it.

She would return, of course. They'd been married twenty-one years. He watched the ferry cast off and start slowly out of the bay. Briefly, he saw his island again, brilliantly sunlit, and Laura in her dark coat walking across its bare stones, the wind blowing her hair, small flowers bright in the stone walls. She would return, and they would have an evening, some kind of day tomorrow, and then they'd go home.

And he would die.

He tilted his hat to shield his face from the sun and closed his eyes, but the darkness of Laura's coat in the bright sunshine remained, a deep, wavering shadow.

"Driscoll, is it?"

Mark's stomach took a mad swoop as he struggled to his feet and took off his hat, the fragility of skin—the skin at Laura's temples, the softness of her stomach—tumbling through his mind. A woman his mother's age stood behind him, on the other side of the low wall. "Yes," he said, "I'm Mark Driscoll."

The sleeves of her sweater were pulled up to her elbows, and she wore a canvas apron; and when she smiled, her false teeth were very white. "You are of course," she said, "with the hat." It was a distinctive hat, brown leather and wide-brimmed, and both of them glanced at it there in his hand. "Your wife is after ringing the shop with a message if we saw you. She's taken a room at Ann Flaherty's for tonight, she says."

He managed to nod as if this made sense, through the insistent memory of the near dampness of Laura's breath against his throat, the texture of her hair against his lips. "Thank you," he said. "Ann Flaherty's."

"It's just up the hill," the woman said. "Not far at all—just past the Spar a bit and to the left. She has a 'Bord Fáilte' sign."

"Ah," he said, and nodded again, suddenly and distinctly aware of a need to urinate. "Well, that's good news."

The woman pushed her hair back from her brow. "There's many open this early now," she said, "before Easter, though they didn't used to. The Germans come earlier every year. But Ann's is a good place—clean and airy, and she's her daughter to help her. She'll look after ye, I'm sure."

"I'm sure she will," he said. "Well, I guess . . ." and smiled and tilted his head toward the town.

"Right past the Spar Market, and to the left," she said, and turned back to the shop.

"Thanks again."

"Oh," she said, "it's a yellow house," and almost at the door of the shop she turned and called, "with the 'Bord Fáilte' sign," and waved.

Well past the turn to the Spar Market, his thighs trembling with weariness, his bladder aching, he stopped to lean against a field wall. He must have misunderstood, in the peculiar vividness of Laura in his mind, or missed a turn in the odd confusion of the village, where none of the streets were straight and everything seemed chaotic. At a picnic table in front of a pub called The American Bar, a middle-aged American man had been explaining loudly to three women (sisters, maybe, their hair, glasses, concerned frowns, and Aran-knit cardigans identical) that all he could figure out was there'd been some kind of crop failure. Two very tall, very blond German men carrying towering backpacks had asked Mark directions. Three children had chased a collie dog almost into him, making him stagger. He'd walked on, slowly, but no B&B had appeared. The sun was still bright but lower, and the wind was still cold. He'd thought to ask the next person he saw for directions, but quite abruptly all the people were gone, left behind in the center of the village with the sandwich shop and the pubs that might have public restrooms, and here he was faced instead with two brown goats, faunlike, side by side, staring at him from the corner of the little field. Beyond them, behind a low wall, stood an abandoned house, its door and windows blocked with stones.

Like a grave, he found himself thinking, like a mausoleum, and he could feel the cold dark of it, and his fear lurched upward into his chest, and he said aloud, "No," and the goats startled and stumbled. He would not fall apart here on the side of the road, would not spiral down into that terror, wet himself, weep—not here, not alone. He drew a deep breath, pinched the bridge of his nose. First things

first: he would walk up behind that house and relieve himself. Then he would walk back down to the village and ask
directions.

He walked slowly up the narrow grassy path between the
fields, touching the tops of the walls for balance. The goats
pivoted to watch him, and he saw that their collars were fastened together. He stepped behind the house, out of view of
the road and the goats. The two windows were blocked with
stone, as in the front, but the wooden back door still hung,
ajar, a rusted water trough beside it. A broken wooden chair
lay in the grass; a pale flowered rag showed in the tangled
grass nearby. It was only a house, a sad, abandoned house,
and he might have imagined its people, but a queer yodeling
cry rose from beyond it, and he saw a woman with a bucket
coming up across a field. If she raised her head, she'd see
him. He opened the door wider, and nearly stumbled over an
escaping yellow cat. "Sorry," he whispered, and looked
inside quickly—just a small room, empty but for a pile of
trash and maybe the remains of a fire by the far wall—
before he stepped in and pulled the door shut.

He had expected it to be dank, and dark: he hadn't
expected such fruity warmth, or so night-blue a darkness, or
the illusion of stars, of being suspended among stars. It
dizzied him, and he put out his hands, as if he might fall.
The stones were packed tight in the other door and in the
four small windows, but tiny specks of light came through:

he understood how the illusion was achieved, but still the stars remained, and for a long moment he stood there with his arms extended, feeling the heavens whirling him slowly, gently, from the known to the unknown.

Then his eyes adjusted to the darkness and the dark grew lighter, the starry points paler; the sound of a bucket hitting stone came to him from outside, and his bladder insisted, so, apologetically, he did what he had come in to do, one hand against the warm dry wall, his gaze elevated to the luminous shadows.

The goats and the woman were gone when he came back around the house, and as he walked back down the grassy path to the road, he saw a boy trotting up the road from town. He recognized him as the tallest of the boys who'd been chasing the dog, and the boy raised his hand and called out, "Mr. Driscoll, you've gone wrong!" grinning as he changed from his steady trot to an exaggerated imitation of exhausted effort. He looked to be about eight.

They met at the road, the boy panting elaborately. Mark smiled and said, "You're absolutely right. What's your name?"

"Oh, I'm Stephen," he said, and put out his hand. "I saw you below."

"I saw you, too. Did you catch that dog?" Stephen's

warm, narrow hand reminded Mark sharply of his own sons, almost men now, grown far past this frankness.

"Ah, no," Stephen said, blushing a little. "We were just messin'."

"Well," Mark said. He understood the blush; apparently people in the village had watched him wander away in the wrong direction. "So I'm lost, trying to find Ann Flaherty's. Can I get there from here?"

The boy didn't register the joke. "You can of course," he said seriously.

"All right. Can you tell me where I go?"

"Will I take you?"

"You don't have to do that."

The boy's seriousness turned worried, and he rubbed his knuckles along his jaw, the gesture of some grown man. "I'm to get you sorted, Mrs. Kilbride said."

"Is that the woman at the sweater shop?"

The grin returned. "Ah, no—that's Mrs. Joyce. Mrs. Kilbride, she's—young." He pursed his lips, his eyes dancing, and Mark almost laughed.

"All right, then—you'll take me," he said. "Let's go," and they walked down the side of the road.

"I saw some goats back there," Mark said. "Their collars were hooked together. Why is that?"

"That way they won't be able to get out."

"Doesn't it keep them from eating, too?"

"Oh, no. There's not a bother on them."

"Do you have goats?"

The boy laughed. "No," he said, and after a few more strides, he said, "Are you American?"

"Yep," Mark said.

"My cousins live in America," Stephen said. "In Chicago. I'll probably go there someday."

"It's quite a city."

"Maybe I'll see you there," Stephen said, giving his grin again.

"Maybe so," Mark said.

"That's if I don't keep up the fishing."

"Is that what your father does?"

"It is. And my brothers." He hopped in front of Mark and hopped back. "So we don't have *goats,*" he said, laughing.

"I see," Mark said. "And is that the best thing about being a fisherman?" They were nearly to the village.

The boy shook his head. "My cousin Dara was drowned once. Now you go on here," he said, and stopped at the turn down what seemed to be a driveway, at the end of which a small parking lot backed a supermarket, "and then there," pointing.

"Ah—so I was supposed to go all the way *to* the Spar Market. That's where I went wrong." The sun was low, and the lane was already dusky.

"He said he saw Little Aran once."

"Your cousin?"

Stephen nodded, and narrowed his eyes at Mark, as if measuring him.

"Little Aran—is that Inisheer?"

"No, it is not," Stephen said, and his tone was so level Mark looked him in the eye.

"Is it an island?" Mark asked carefully.

"It is," Stephen said. "A magic island."

Mark nodded slowly. "I see," he said.

The boy looked away, rubbed his jaw again, and then grinned. "Yeah—all right, then—down the left there and it's Ann Flaherty's, and you're sorted," and he turned before Mark could offer to shake his hand again, and trotted away. But then he stopped and called back, "She's not young!"

He was right: curiosity and disapproval balanced in the not-young, thin, sharp face of Ann Flaherty. She glared at his hat as she opened the door and let him in, and instead of hello she said, "She's gone off to The American Bar."

"Thank you," Mark said, and if she could be abrupt, he could match her. "I'd like to see our room."

"You're sick, I'd say."

"I have been," he said.

She twisted her mouth and turned and led him down the narrow hall to a remarkably pleasant room. Laura's scarf lay on the bed. "It's en suite," she said, pointing to a door, "and there's more blankets in there," pointing to a wardrobe.

He nodded, and picked up the scarf and folded it into a small square and put it into his coat pocket.

"It'll be cold, now the sun's gone," Ann Flaherty said, and then, grudgingly, "They've music there tonight." She wasn't young, and she wasn't pretty, but Mark could imagine the texture of her thin, dry lips against his own, and for a second he was light-headed with the temptation to touch her.

Instead he smiled and asked, "Where exactly is this American Bar from here?"

Her smile was sour and satisfied. "Up the lane and down the hill," she said.

"Thank you," he said. She turned, and he followed her back down the hall.

At the door she said, "She's got the key."

He put his hat back on. "All right," he said, and went out into the growing dusk to find his wife.

She sat alone at one of the picnic tables on the deserted lawn in front of The American Bar, looking down toward the bay, where a few boats showed small lights. Mark stood still, watching her; she raised her glass, drank, and set it down again on the table. The wind was much less now, and he could hear the murmur of talk from inside the pub. He inhaled carefully, and then walked across the rough grass to the end of her table.

"Hi," he said.

She didn't look up, but after a small pause she said, "Hi."

The island never appeared to Mark again, and he never told Laura about seeing it, or about whirling among the miraculous stars in the abandoned house. But that night, taking a seat across from her at that picnic table, as carefully as if this were some crucial moment of courtship, every gesture perilous, choices still unmade, he said, "I hear there's going to be music in there."

"So they say," she said.

He touched the scarf in his pocket and reached tentatively for her glass. She slid it toward him, and he took a sip.

"I met a kid today," he said. "He told me about this island we might want to see sometime." He passed the glass back to her, and left his hand beside it, so when she took it again, her fingers brushed his.

"Where is it?"

"Pretty near here," he said. "There's seals there."

Inside, the music began, a swaying fiddle.

It was nearly dark, but he could see the pale line of her

jaw, and the way she lifted her chin. "I'd like to see seals," she said. "Next year we should go there."

He nodded. "That's what I thought," he said.

They shared the rest of the pint slowly, without talking, and when it was gone she shrugged her shoulders quickly and said, "It's getting cold," and he took the scarf from his pocket and held it out to her, and when she took it, he moved his fingertips softly against her palm. He watched her hold the scarf up and let it unfold, and swirl it in the dark air above her head and let it settle across her shoulders, and bend her head and lift her hair free of it.

6

EVENING

Pretend it's a story, and pretend it ends like this:

On the afternoon of her husband's sixty-ninth birthday, as the day's brief light gave way to dusk (it was December again, as it seemed to her it so often was, now), as she walked quickly along Dominick Street toward the center of Galway, where she meant to buy wrapping paper for his present and then stop in McDonagh's on her way back for take-away cod to reheat for their supper, Mary veered to the right around a woman with a double pram and bumped into the man of her dreams.

It was only a small collision. She hadn't been charging along, for all her sense of hurry, and he didn't exactly dart out the door of Monroe's, coming out half backward, his hand raised in farewell to someone inside. She didn't have

any parcels yet for his elbow to send flying, and he had no
stack of important papers for the wind to catch and scatter
as he turned and put out his hands to steady her and apologize, so it wasn't dramatic at all: just two people in late middle age, wearing winter coats, jostling each other on the
crowded pavement.

"Sorry," he said, half his wits still inside the pub with
John Foley and the other half fuddled by embarrassment.

"It's all right," she said, half her wits still hurrying ahead
to Pound City where the birthday paper was every bit as
nice, and half not fancying at all coming face to face with a
fellow bumbling out of a pub in the darkening afternoon.

Because they were face to face now, after exactly two
years, face to face and his hands on her arms, and their
eyes met—in life, as in stories, eyes may speak, and theirs
said surprise and then joy and then shyness, and in that
instant between joy and shyness only the tailoring of winter coats, which prevents free movement of the arms, kept
him from gathering her to him, kept her from reaching to
touch his face.

"Mary," he said.

Beneath the noise of the traffic passing and the rush and
chatter of people passing, she heard birdsong, and the low
lapping of lake water.

"Eamon, is it you?" she said.

"It is," he said. "Ah, Mary, you're looking great."

"You're looking fine yourself—New York agrees with you."

He released her arms and said, "How's the little dog?" and then the street was real for her again, and the cod and the gift wrap, and her husband at home with the dog waiting for her return, and Eamon, after all this time, was himself only real, only a man she'd thought of sometimes and who had walked, now and then, through her dreams.

"Ah, she's grand—smart as can be, and a sweet temper, you know."

"I do," he said, "the lovely Lady," and she knew he was pleased. "I've moved house, in New York, and so I've a dog there now, another like her, the longhaired dachshund." He went on and said he liked the States, all in all, his grandsons were fine, his son doing well, and he'd been out west the once to visit his daughter.

Mary said her younger son would be coming over from Cleveland in February, when the fares were low, and the older one, who had a bit more money, had been over twice this year already, in May and November, from Indianapolis, though he'd had trouble getting out in November because of weather, and had they had such a bad winter in New York this year?

"Not so bad, not so bad," he said, and then—she had no idea what the color in her cheeks did for her eyes, there in the dusk of the winter street—he ducked his head and took a great breath and said, as if he were surprised at it, "I'm getting married on Monday."

"Are you really?"

He laughed and said, "I am! To a woman from Costelloe, for all I met her in Brooklyn."

"Costelloe," Mary said. "That's lovely, Eamon—it's lovely for you, not to be alone anymore. I'm sure she's wonderful, isn't she?"

"She is—Alice is her name," he said, and that she was a widow for many years, living with her daughter in Brooklyn, and she was with her own people today, and his sons were coming from Dublin tonight and they'd go out to Costelloe on Sunday, and all be back in Brooklyn by week's end.

"But ye'll not go back and live in the city?"

"We will," he said. "The children are there, and we're used to it, you know."

"It's good ye've the dog, then—it's good to have a pet, all the same, if ye must live in the city," she said. She made an adjustment of her purse on her arm, and she said, "I wish you happiness. It's great running into you," and they both laughed.

"It is," he said. "Well, you've places to go," he said, "and I've the train to meet."

"Good-bye," she said. "Have a safe trip, and a happy new year to ye both—God bless," and she patted his arm and they parted.

And pretend, if it ends like that, that it began like this, just over two years earlier:

As the lights came up in Taibhdhearc, the Irish-language theater, for the interval of *Fiddler on the Roof,* the winter theatrical presented by Colaiste na Coiribe, the Irish-language secondary school, and featuring Mary's grand-nieces Hannah and Molly as the younger daughters, several children began carrying the raffle prizes around the curtain and arranging them at the edge of the stage, and Lyle said, "Well, the kid's no Zero Mostel."

"He's a schoolboy," Mary said. "I think they're doing beautifully."

"I still say it's a funny choice—bunch of Irish Catholic kids pretending to be Russian Jews."

"What difference does that make?" Mary said. She really didn't understand him at all, sometimes. "They've got to pretend to be somebody. The music's lovely."

"Could be," he said.

She folded her hands in her lap.

They'd lived in Ireland more than a year, and he still criticized everything, from the weather to the state of the pavement to the weight of the coins, and she was sick to death of hearing it from him about every little thing. He hadn't wanted to come tonight, and she'd said he needn't, and he'd said could she return the tickets and she'd said no, and he'd said, Well there you are, and anyway, if I don't go, you and your sister will just talk all night about if I had any family feeling *at all at all,* I'd be there. She hated it when he mocked the Irish way of talking so she'd said, Well, we'd be right if we did, and had left him standing in the kitchen and had gone upstairs to clean the bathroom. Then he'd come to the foot of the stairs and shouted for her as if she'd gone way out the country, and hadn't answered when she'd said, What is it, so she'd had to go down the stairs and into the sitting room and say it again, and then he'd said, I suppose the thing's in Irish since it's in that place (he pretended he didn't know how to say the name of the theater, though she'd explained it—Tyve-yark, very easy if you didn't look at it), and she'd said of course it wasn't, and he'd said he'd go, then, just to keep the peace.

And this was what he called keeping the peace.

What she should have done, she thought, staring at her hands, was say yes, she could return his ticket, and then she could have come with Róisín. If she had, they'd be hurrying, now, out to the lobby for a cup of tea, and saying how adorable the children were, and how well they sang, and how impressive the raffle prizes were; they'd be eager to get their tea and get back in time for the drawing to begin, and they might even buy a few more raffle tickets in the lobby, since they'd both seen the Galway crystal vase brought out.

The evening that could have gone like that hovered just off to the side, as if it actually existed, and that sense of possibility brought with it patience enough that when Lyle said, "How many raffle tickets did you get?" she could say, "Twenty," as pleasantly as if she hadn't just a moment ago felt temper stinging her cheeks. She took them from her purse, eight green and twelve blue, and she gave him his choice; he took half of each, though he'd tell anybody that gambling was a waste of money, and a raffle was gambling, whatever you called it. Herself, she knew the school made more on the raffle than on the show itself, and she was glad to help with a few pounds, though she'd never in her life won a thing.

The man came out with the box of tickets and the little boy to draw them, and Mary leaned forward a bit.

"Oh, Jesus," Lyle growled, "they're doing the damned thing in Irish."

They were, of course, but they'd do it after in English—everything in Taibhdhearc they did that way, including when they announced where the fire exits were, and he knew that as well as she did, but she couldn't for the life of her think of a civil way to say it to him, so she just clutched her purse with both hands as if she were actually in danger of slapping him. And of course he never said a word when the man repeated his announcement in English and said he'd be doing all the numbers in English now, because he was embarrassed to admit that numbers in Irish had never come easy for him. But the audience laughed—as if, like Mary, they remembered their own struggles with Irish—and the first ticket was drawn and the number called, and a sweet little girl, no more than six years old, came running down the aisle with her ticket in her hand, to choose from the great heap of prizes.

She wanted the huge white stuffed bear—anybody could see that, the way she crouched there and nearly touched the plaid bow about its neck—but the audience began shouting, "The crystal! Take the crystal!" The vase was the grandest of the prizes, but Mary's heart went out to the girleen: if she took the crystal, she'd give it to her mother, of course, and never be let touch it again, and the winning would be the end of it, with nothing of her own to remember it by. She did take it, at last, and the audience applauded, and a big boy—her brother—met her as she stepped off the stage, and he carried the crystal up the aisle for her, and the raffle went on. The next winner was a teacher from the school, and when he chose the brandy the place went mad with laughter, and he played at staggering his way back to his seat. Then it was on to the baskets of cheeses or biscuits, the toys and the jewelry and perfume

and the odd book, with applause and advice for every winner, cheers and laughter for some. Mary's anger with Lyle
had passed in her sympathy with the child, but she found
she couldn't quite shake the sadness that sympathy had
brought—as if she herself had been disappointed, and not
the girl—and she was relieved when the pile of prizes was
nearly gone, only a box of inexpensive sweets and a bottle
of aftershave left: she was ready to see the sad half of the
play, and then go home, and wake tomorrow with a better
view of the world.

"That's you," Lyle said. "Green 725—that's you!"

"No," she said.

"Yes, it is, look—" and he was pointing at the green
ticket, and she could see the number, and the fellow on the
stage repeated it, and then Lyle gave her arm a nudge, a
push, and he said again, "Go on—it's you."

Again she said, "No," as calmly and firmly as she'd ever
said a word, and then she glared at the aftershave and the
sweets until the fellow said he'd have to go to another number, and he did, and someone else took the sweets, and
finally someone else took the aftershave.

Mary herself, who, in fact, never said a thing about it to
anyone, would have said it began later, the day she met
Eamon, like this:

Mary knew this about Christmas: the finding of the gifts needed a bit of magic about it or it became merely shopping. So when she found herself, in midafternoon on the day after American Thanksgiving, the biggest shopping day of the American year, standing at the window of the Treasure Chest, staring at the holly-decked display of the same Galway crystal that had been heart-decked in February and shamrock-decked in March, wishing she were back in Cleveland with its dozen shopping malls, she knew it was time to call it a day and go home, even though she hadn't yet found a thing for the sons of her sister's husband's niece, and they were the only little children she had to shop for this year.

And she knew this about being blue: if you gave in to it, it only got worse. So when she discovered herself trudging along Father Griffin Road resenting the weight of the holly-printed shopping bag of gifts she hadn't really wanted to buy, and discovered that she was dreading going home to Lyle who'd say, again, that she ought to go to Dublin, for crying out loud, if she couldn't find what she wanted in Galway, because he simply didn't understand that if she couldn't find what she wanted in Galway they might as well give it up and move back to Ohio—he didn't see that there was something wrong with her if she couldn't have a happy Christmas in the city where she'd been a child—when she found that she was in utter misery with the tears springing to her eyes and most of a mile left to walk in the damp gray cold of this December day, she absolutely stopped right there outside the chemist's, just past the little park, and told herself to snap out of it. She put down her shopping bag and found a tissue in her purse and blew her nose. When she looked up from doing that, she saw, just there, the beautifully steamy window of Anton's, a little restaurant where she and Lyle sometimes had lunch because he liked their soups: beautifully steamy, the people inside bright blurred shapes of color, the light through the steam looking like coziness itself. There now, she said to herself. You just go right in there and treat yourself to a cup of his good coffee—with cream, thank you, the likes of which Ohio has never known—and a piece of his chocolate cake with the orange sauce, and you'll be out of this mood and fit to live with humans in the world.

And so she took herself through the door, where the illusion of coziness disappeared immediately: the small room was both drafty and overheated, and so crowded with tables that Mary barely had room to step in and let the door close behind her. The colorful blurs became pale people hunched alone or in pairs or huddled in sour-faced groups; there wasn't a table to spare, and nobody looked inclined to move their books or parcels aside to let her take one of the few empty chairs.

But a piece of cake came by just then, carried by a slim waitress who had two cups of coffee in her other hand, and she passed close enough that Mary could smell the orange, and the girl smiled and said, "You're welcome—there's a place for you just there," gesturing with her chin toward the last table at the back where someone sat reading a newspaper. So Mary smiled, too, and made her way between the tables to that one at the back, a way so hampered by her shopping bag and purse and the coats draped on the backs of chairs that the same waitress had returned to the kitchen and come back with a slice of fruit tart and a fresh pot of tea for the fellow with the newspaper by the time Mary reached the table.

"There now," the girl said, setting down the plate and pot and picking up his empty soup bowl and plate, "will I get you anything more?"

"Ah, no," he said, "I'm grand," and he smiled at Mary as he folded his newspaper and put it aside. He was a man about her own age.

"You don't mind?" Mary said.

"Not at all," he said. He poured his tea.

"You're very good," Mary said, and then, to the waitress, "I'd like a coffee with cream, please, and the chocolate cake." She set her bag down and slipped off her coat.

"With cream?" the girl inquired.

"Coffee with cream," Mary agreed.

"Cream with the cake, too?" the girl explained.

"It's great with the cream," the man advised.

"Then cream with the cake, too," Mary declared. She moved her shopping bag against the wall, draped her coat over it, and sat down across from the man.

"You're after bringing home the Christmas early," he said, nodding toward the bag.

She'd wonder later what it was in his face or voice that invited her so. Gentleness, she'd think, or a shy openness, or something so deeply familiar in his words themselves that she felt immediately they could speak as neighbors, nearly as friends. Later still, she'd wonder if it was that at all, or just the shape of the wool scarf at his neck or the tweed of his jacket, so like her father's jacket from long ago, or the calm size of his country man's hands as he cut his tart with the edge of his fork—but in this moment she simply felt welcomed and easy, so she said, "I suppose I am, but the spirit's not in it."

He nodded, chewing, and then swallowed and said, "I've the same trouble now the children are grown and the grandchildren so far away."

"That's it, isn't it—Christmas—the presents and all—it's for the children, really."

"You have children?"

"I do—two sons, grown now, living in America."

"I've two in America, and two still in Ireland," he said.

"The grandchildren are all over there. Two boys in Brooklyn, and two girls and a boy in Seattle."

"I envy you," she said. "Mine are in no hurry even to marry. Do you get over there to see them?"

"In summer," he said, and ate another bite of his tart. "It's fine to see them then, when their school term is over, but it's not like having young ones, and Santa Claus." He grinned, a bit sheepish, she thought. "I'm just after getting myself a little dog to keep me company at home—I suppose I might hang a stocking for her this year."

"You've the two children still here, though—there'll be more grandchildren."

He shook his head and blushed. "The daughter's a nun with the Poor Clares, and the youngest boy—he's in Dublin. I don't know about him."

"It's lovely your daughter's a nun," Mary said. "I have a cousin that's a nun," and then she was blushing, too, catching what he might have meant about his son, and then ashamed of herself for thinking it, and then ashamed of being ashamed, and they were both grateful the girl came back then with the cake and coffee. When she left them, Mary said, carefully, "I loved Christmas when my boys were small."

"Maybe," he said, a certain caution in his voice, too, "it's the little children keep us right—keep the magic in it for *us.*" He lifted his cup and looked at its rim. "They keep us trying for it," he said, but then he shook his head and sipped the tea.

She could see he wasn't satisfied with what he'd said, so she just nodded, and tasted her cake, and waited for him to go on, holding quiet in her mind that he'd said "magic" in such an ordinary way, as if he, too, thought it was a thing that could be spoken of, sought. Needed, in ordinary life. The cake was lovely.

He set his cup down. "When we were children, now, it wasn't so much about the presents as about the church," he said, and before she could nod in agreement—everyone said this, and she thought it must be so—he chuckled, and added, "Or so I think now, if I'm careful what I remember."

"I loved visiting the crib in the church, and taking the bit of straw for luck," Mary said. She sprinkled a packet of sugar over the whipped cream on her coffee and watched it melt in. For a second, she almost could smell the straw mixed with the rest of the church smell, but then it was gone. "I remember the presents, though they were always small little things. Simple. One year a china baby that fit in my pocket. Oh, I thought she was perfect!" She looked up at him and smiled. "If you're *not* careful, what do you remember?"

He smiled, too. "There was a box of paints one year. Ten squares of color in the flat tin box, with a design pressed in them. I loved it so much I couldn't bear to use it. I don't know if I ever did, but I remember my mother saying I didn't seem too keen on it, and I couldn't think how to tell her what it was." He poured the last of his tea; his plate was empty. "There's a sadness to the best of memories," he said, as if he were apologizing, or as if it were an old saying, its proof in its age.

"Ah, there is," Mary said. She touched her cup. "You've put me in mind of a little delft tea set I got one year, and broke the little pot the very day."

He stirred a drop of milk into his tea and then laid the spoon down and took up his fork and tidied his plate as he talked. "One autumn myself and my brother went into the town to school for a few weeks, with our cousins—maybe when my sister was being born. We lived out the country, so those few weeks in town I remember like they were a year." He was pushing the flakes of pastry into a line. "We'd heard of a big Christmas party given in the castle there for the village children, and we kept imagining we'd be invited along, though we'd gone home weeks before that. It didn't happen, of course."

"Not the castle in Oranmore?" she said, and when he nodded, she said, "I was a girl in Oranmore!"

"Ah, you never were!"

They both laughed, each searching the other's face now for something identifiable.

"I was Mary Curtin," Mary offered. "I was a bit older

when we went out there—eleven—but my brothers were younger, Thomas and James and John?"

He shook his head. "I'm Eamon Bennett, but I'd say I'm older than yourself, and so I'd not have been in school with your brothers either."

"Had you a cousin Charlie? My brothers knew a boy Charlie Bennett."

But again he shook his head. Embarrassed not to have been acquainted all those years ago, as if they'd both mis-represented their residence in Oranmore, both of them looked to their cups, and it was a long moment before he cleared his throat and, without looking up, said, "Did ye go to the party at the castle?"

"Once," she said, and with the saying of that word, the party came back strong, the children around the grand table, the pretty decorations and the great tree all aglimmer—and herself standing back, seeing the fruitcake with the silver decorations in the frosting, and the big eyes of the children shining, and how she'd nearly wept then, awkward in her sister's dress, knowing she'd got too old for such magic, at only thirteen. "It wasn't so grand as you might have thought," she said, quite harshly. Hearing herself, she looked him in the face again and said, "Do you still live out the country there?"

"I do, for now. I raised my children there in the same house, but now they're grown and gone—" He raised his hand for their going, and laid it back on the table. "I've a few sheep, some bees—I sell a bit of honey. My wife died a long time back. Most of the old families have died or sold their places and moved into town. It's daft to try to keep a farm all on your own." Now it was his voice that had gone hard, though his face wouldn't take the tone.

"You've the dog," she said, trying for a weak joke.

At last, it seemed to her, he smiled. "I do, and she'll be wondering what's kept me in town so long, when I said I'd just get my messages and be back." He moved his chair away from the table.

"I'm glad to have met you, Eamon," she said.

"You've brightened the day," he said, standing, and then he put out his hand to her across the table they'd shared, and his hand was warm and gentle when she took it. "I'd say you'll find your Christmas spirit in time."

"Ah, I will," she said, and felt herself blushing again. "It's just a mood."

He let go her hand and took his cap from where it hung on the back of his chair, a cap that could have been her father's, her brother's, out there years ago in Oranmore. "The holly, now," he said. "You might try searching for some and see if that's the cure, with an angel dancing on every point."

She laughed. "I'd look a right fool out tramping the country for holly!"

"You'd look great," he said, and so they were both smiling as he left the table and went to the counter and paid.

A few minutes later—her coffee had gone cold, and with the cream the cake was a bit too much—when Mary put her coat back on and took up her bag again and went to the same counter, she found he'd paid for her treat as well, which flattered her, and as she walked on home she thought he was a very tidy man, for a widower, very neat about himself, and sad, for all his good humor and generosity.

Wherever it began, if it's to be a story, there must be a middle, and the middle here may be very simple. Between the evening she refused her raffle prize and the day she met Eamon, Mary imagined often, as she seldom had before, that she might never have gone to America. She could have stayed in Ireland, and married, and had a life like other women had, without all the disruption of America, and an American husband, and sons who were Americans, and then all this complication of coming back and Lyle's being dissatisfied. And between the day she met Eamon and the next time she saw him, that imagined other life began to be set on an Irish farm, with her other self an Irish wife to an Irish husband, with nine bean rows in the garden and a hive for the honeybees, and sometimes she found herself nearly pretending Eamon as that Irish husband.

Two weeks before Christmas, in Dublin, looking at plaid woolen scarves, considering whether the softer scarves would wear as well as the others, she knew, but pretended she didn't, that Lyle would never want such a thing.

A few days later, when Lyle read out a bit from the newspaper about the high profit in cut flowers, and chuckled in a mean way and said Jimmy ought to think about becoming a florist, she said, as she always did, that Jimmy would find his own way in time, he needn't be concerned. That started them, as it always did, on the old worn quarrel about their younger son; behind the words of that quarrel, as if those words were only a thin veil between herself and another life, she could nearly see Eamon putting out his hand to greet his youngest boy, who lived in Dublin—for the least instant, she could feel the texture of Eamon's jacket, as if she'd just had her hand on his arm.

Two days after Christmas, as she rolled out crust for an apple pie, she wondered if the poor fellow often ate his meals in restaurants, for the company. She pictured him alone at a table in a kitchen that was like the kitchen she'd left in Oranmore, though she knew if he'd raised a family in his house, the kitchen would have been modernized sometime. Still, she let him sit there for a bit, at the bare wooden table with the fire off to the left and the lonely peace of the place dropping slow through the lamplight, and the smell of sliced apples hung in the air there, too, as if she were at the other end of the table from him, making this tart, and he waiting to have it warm with his tea.

So pretend that's the middle: Mary pretending, an innocent thing, a comfort, a little habit that gives her patience with the reality. Pretend Mary is a sensible woman, well aware of the difference between fact and fiction, and that she knows, in her deep heart's core, that this half dream of another life in a small farmhouse in a bee-loud glade is just a fantasy she'd never choose in real life—she's fond of shops and plumbing and dependable heating and a predictable income, and Lyle. Pretend that for Christmas she gives him two shirts, one of them blue to bring out his eyes, and a set of gardening tools he has admired, and a fancy garden-planning system of notebooks and grids, and that, for his birthday, she has chosen with great care an atlas, because the one they have was bought years ago when the boys were small, and he grumbles about it when he looks up someplace he's come across in the newspaper and the country isn't there.

And pretend it all comes together when Mary sees Eamon again, like this:

On the morning of her husband's sixty-seventh birthday, during a rare sunny patch, as she stood on the shingle of

Claddagh Quay feeding the swans stale bread from the bag she'd brought from home and half pretending she stood in the yard of a farmhouse feeding her own chickens, Mary heard her name called and looked up and saw Eamon coming toward her, his cap in his hand and a little brown dog on a leash.

She raised her hand and smiled, and went back to tossing the bits of bread to the swans. He came, as if it were the most natural thing in the world, and stood beside her, and the dog sat beside him, the greedy swans with their stony eyes crowding the water before them, mute and demanding.

A long moment passed, and then he flicked his cap against his thigh and gestured with the cap toward the swans. "Cheeky lot."

She laughed, and after a few more moments she looked at him there, and said, "Did you hang the stocking for the little dog, then?"

In answer he put his cap back on his head and glared at the swans before he said, as if she'd challenged or accused him somehow, "I went to mass."

Her face went hot and she looked away. There it was, that was what men were like, no matter their country, and she'd been imagining a creature that wasn't in nature, and anything she might say—Did you now? or You did of course— or anything she might do—laugh, or dump the rest of the bread and leave—would be foolish, or just wrong.

"I'm taking the dog to the vet," he said, in the same offended tone, and then his voice went somehow thicker as he spoke faster, "and it's not the thing I'd choose to do but it's no easy thing to do the right thing in the world—" He cleared his throat and went on, "You'd think there'd be a fellow in the whole of Connaught—" and then, at last, the bitterness fell away, and he said, "Ah, Mary, I'd no idea."

She was looking at him again now, of course, and when he turned and met her eyes, his were full of tears.

"Eamon?" she said.

"It's my son in Brooklyn," he said.

Her realization that she had never in her life as a woman kissed an Irish man was distant and sad, and only the fact that near strangers don't do such things, in late middle age, in public places, late in December, on the mornings of their husbands' birthdays, kept her from putting her hand out and touching his sad face. Instead, while he found his handkerchief and pressed it to his eyes and then turned away to blow his nose, she turned the bag up and dumped the rest of the bread onto the ground, tucked the bag itself into her purse, and took his arm. "We might walk down the prom a bit," she said, and he nodded.

He had started near the end of the story he had to tell, a story that began just after they'd met in Anton's, a story full of Eamon's ideas about fathers and sons, about keeping farms that didn't pay, about holiday homes and the future of

Ireland, but it came down to this: his son in New York had asked him to come and live with him there, to be with the grandsons when both parents were traveling for their jobs; at the same time, a chance had come to sell the farm, to a tourism concern that meant to put in holiday homes; it was daft to try to keep a farm all on your own, and he wasn't the young man he'd once been. He'd sold the sheep and bees, and a month ago he'd booked his flight to America for early tomorrow. All that was grand, but he'd advertised the dog free to a good home for these three weeks and had not a single reply. They'd come to a bench and sat down, looking out toward Mutton Island and its little lighthouse. "It's the holidays, I suppose," he said, "but there it is—I've no choice I can see but to take her out to the vet and hope he'll know someone." He leaned down and unhooked the dog's leash. The dog looked up at him and tilted her head and wrinkled her brow, as if she were trying to be certain of his meaning. He laid his hand on the dog's small head. "You're grand," he said, "you're grand," and he looked out over the bay and then back into the dog's eyes. "Get on," he said, and the dog turned and ran for the water.

"The water's very cold," Mary said.

"Watch," he said, and they sat together and watched the little dog charge the waves and then leap back, again and again.

Mary said it would be grand for him to be with his family,

and he agreed, and said he was glad to be free of the farm, really, though he knew he'd miss it sometimes; Mary mentioned his children in Ireland, and he said the boy in Dublin had decided to go to London and, maybe, in a year or two, to New York. And then Mary asked what the dog's name was, and he said Lady, and smiled the saddest smile she thought she'd ever seen and said Lovely Lady, and Mary said would he write down his address in Brooklyn so she could write and tell him when she'd found a home for Lady.

Walking home with the little dog trotting willingly beside her, she explained to herself, as she meant to explain to Lyle, that Fionnuala, with the two little boys and the house out on the Tuam Road, might very well want a dog for them, and if she didn't, maybe the old fellow who'd just taken the house next to Róisín would be looking for company, and if he didn't, why, it wouldn't kill them to advertise for a home for the poor creature and keep her themselves in the meantime. She imagined she might have to get on her high horse, as he called it, and insist, but there was no need to have the little dog put down just because of timing: she was well trained and pleasant and given a bit of time someone would want her.

What she didn't imagine, what she'd never have pretended, was Lyle's face when she came in the door and he saw the dog—he'd been scowling, probably because she'd been gone a bit longer than he'd expected and his lunch would be a bit later than usual, and then he saw the dog and Mary nearly laughed aloud at the confusion that went across his mouth and eyes before he looked into Mary's own eyes with such timid pleasure she was reminded of Lyle thirty years and more before, Lyle a young man and shy and awkward and fancying her. "A dog?" he said now.

"Her name's Lady," Mary said, and then she just watched Lyle bend down and lay his hand on the dog's small head, and watched the dog look into his face, and wrinkle her brow and tilt her head.

When he stood again, he ran both hands over his cheeks and cleared his throat. "Well," he said, "I didn't expect a dog, I'll admit. Lady, huh?"

One night, months later, in the summer, as she lay in bed waiting for sleep after she and Lyle had quarreled over some small thing, she pretended she'd never left Ireland and lived now on an Irish farm out the country, and she found that she couldn't tell whether the man she pretended walking across the yard toward the house in the twilight was Eamon or Lyle, or her father, or one of her brothers. Fair enough, she thought. Fair enough, and, because she was still out of patience with Lyle, she thought, Less different than chalk and cheese, at the end of the day, and after a while she slept.

Because for Mary, of course, this isn't a story; it's just her life. So after she and Eamon part, there on the pavement, in the dusk, for the last time, she'll get her wrapping paper, and she and Lyle (she was already thinking of him, by the time she'd crossed Wolfe Tone Bridge and turned up Quay Street, hurrying again, a little behind her time now, thinking as she did every year how hard it must have been for him as a child to have his birthday the week after Christmas, and whether she might get the cod now because by the time she got back the queue would be long), they'll have their supper, and she'll give him the aftershave she had Jimmy find in Cleveland and the outdoor thermometer, and their lives will go on.

7

But Come Ye Back

The wall that joins the two houses is so thick that sounds rarely pass through, but tonight Mary Sullivan hears the crying of a baby on the other side. It is the ordinary fretful crying of a baby waking in the night, familiar still to Mary although her own children are men now. If they cry now in the night, it is not for her, or no longer hers to comfort, and they are far away, Kevin and Jimmy, an ocean away, from where she sits, wrapped in a blanket against the chills that come and go, in the rocking chair in the guest room she keeps for her sons' visits, and waits for someone to come and comfort the crying child. She has come away from her bed into this room to give Lyle a chance to sleep even if she can't, and she is sitting up because her cough is worse when she lies down. She wants to sleep, her fever makes her drowsy and this cough has kept her from real rest for nearly a week, and she had thought that maybe, sitting up, in the guest room, in the deep silence of midnight, sleep would come to her.

If she could sleep one night, she is sure, she would be on the mend, and her real life would return, she would be again the able woman she has been for so long, the woman who, three weeks ago, dressed and walked through the early-morning streets of Galway to the train station, where her sister Róisín met her and the two of them boarded the 7:45 for a day in Dublin. She came back that day with a slight cold, she thought, that turned out to be a flu, that has settled in her chest. She hasn't been well enough since to call by to welcome the new neighbors, the family whose baby is crying, and she doesn't know whether the baby is a boy or a girl. She took a taxi to mass on Sunday, but since then she hasn't had the energy to go to the shops, and she's had to ask Lyle to go, and she forgets to put on the list things she'd remember to pick up if she could go herself, her real self, the one for whom a walk was a delight in any weather, for whom the sound of the vacuum cleaner wasn't a torture, the Mary who thought about other people and looked forward to the small tasks and pleasures of ordinary days.

She coughs again, a long series of weary coughs. She isn't a woman given to self-pity, but in a distant way she feels sorry for her chest and ribs and stomach, having to endure this again.

Across the hall, alone in their bed, Lyle hears the cough

and braces himself against it, as if it were his own. He wishes, without forming the wish with words, that it were his cough, that he, not his wife, were sick. He wishes this not because he loves her, although he does, although he is seldom aware that he does. He wishes this because the sound of her coughing nearly overwhelms him with a dread that he refuses to recognize as familiar still, although his boyhood as the only child of a widowed mother who coughed is now long past, and his mother's stroke and extended illness and death are now long past, and Mary has never in his life with her been so ill. He is neither heroic nor selfless; if he were coughing, as Mary has been for a week, he would be peevish and demanding, but he is not coughing. He is lying alone in his bed, rigid with dread, in exactly the way he lay alone in his bed as a young man more than forty years ago waiting for his mother's stroke-damaged voice to summon him to his helplessness beside her bed. He does not form with words his wish that the cough leave Mary and lodge in his own chest, he does not form with words his fear. In words he thinks, This has gone on long enough, this is stupid: tomorrow she's seeing a doctor, whether she likes it or not.

Tonight, as she lifted their plates from the table and turned to put them on the counter beside the sink, she swayed, tilted, and the plates clattered from her hand into the sink. He stood, his chair tipping back, and reached for her, but she patted his arm and said, No, no—I'm fine so.

I'm grand. Her hand on his arm was ember hot. Will I make you a cup of tea, she said, and he said, No, thanks.

He by God said no to that, to her carrying the tray into the sitting room.

Lying in his bed, Lyle strikes his own chest with his knuckles, willing Mary's cough to cease, willing her to health.

Mary's coughing stops, and she hears that the baby's crying has risen beyond fretting to need. She stands up from her chair and lets the blanket fall, and without deciding, without really thinking, she steps in the dark to go to the baby who is crying beyond the wall, because her fever has continued to rise and in this moment she does not remember the wall.

Outside this house in the night it is June, and dew is gathering on all the grasses, on the leaves of the many hedges, on the cool stone of the many walls of Galway and on the tiny flowering plants that grow in the crevices of those walls. The dew makes no sound in its gathering, no bird stirs yet, there is no sound at all outside this house save the distant curling of the sea resting in Galway Bay, and overhead the stars are wide and alive.

Lyle hears first the silence that follows the coughing, and then the sound of her rising. He lifts his head to hear more clearly. The sound of her is clumsy somehow.

Across an ocean and across half a continent, where it is

still early evening, their older son Kevin, stretched on his couch to watch the news, raises his head in exactly the same way, and three hundred miles east of him their younger son Jimmy lifts his head too from the pillow, his nap before work ended: by some chance they are all listening when Mary hears a murmur of voice through the wall, and she remembers the wall, and she hears the crying stop. They are all listening, but they do not hear her say God bless, because she cannot quite draw breath enough yet to whisper, and only Lyle, already out of bed and hurrying, his flesh and bones electric with panic, hears her fall.

Lyle had never seen such an emptiness as their street once
the ambulance turned the corner and was gone from his
sight. Its flashing light there in front of the house had made
of walls and leaves and parked cars a harsh, pulsing tableau,
so unfamiliar it seemed the light created the things it illumi-
nated, and now that it was gone nothing but the darkness
remained. He stood in the middle of it, in the street, his
hands loose at his sides. He could feel the quiet settling itself
back into place, filling the holes in the silence the ambulance
men had made with their quick voices and the sharp noises
of their doors, the clang of the metal stretcher against his
own gate. That gate, and beyond it the door to his empty
house, stood open behind him.

No, not empty. Lyle hunched his shoulders once and let
them drop again. He could feel in the air at his back how the
house was not empty at all, but shimmering still with the
scraps of emergency: the rocking chair pushed into the hall,
the dented shade of the blue lamp, the blanket sprawled on
the floor.

If he walked back into the house now he would walk back
into the sound of her falling. He would half see how she lay

on her back when he came through the door and shouted, and would feel in his throat the dull horror of her lying there unmoved by his voice. His weakness would be waiting for him, the trembling of his hands on the telephone receiver, and his panting as he spoke to the man who answered, and the groan of her unconscious breathing filling the room as he waited there beside her and how he held her hand not to comfort her but to keep himself from running down the stairs to make the ambulance come faster and the smell of his own body from inside his pajamas as he crouched there beside her, her glasses crooked on her face and his fear of touching her face to straighten them, his fear.

The ambulance men had brought it to order. They had moved the chair, righted the lamp. They had talked quietly to him as he led them up the stairs, asking her age and general health, how long she'd been sick, how recently she'd eaten, and then, "This is a convenient house, in't it, walk to everything—city center, the bay," one of them said, and the other, "Solid, too—these older ones are. Have ye lived here long?"

"Five years," and his voice, like theirs, was quiet, a kind of casual. "We moved here from Ohio, in the States."

"I thought you were American."

"Your man Bill Clinton played a bit of golf at Bally-bunion last month."

In the guest room, they spoke in the same calm voices to

Mary, explaining who they were and what they were doing, even though she didn't respond, and to one another, reminding and agreeing, and all the while they were taking her blood pressure and starting oxygen and an IV, unfolding a blanket and then lifting her onto the stretcher. "We'll be taking her to Casualty at University Hospital," the first one said, and she was tidy, asleep, tucked into their blanket. They fastened the buckles to hold her that way. They lifted the stretcher. "You know where it is?" the second one said. "Yes," Lyle said. "Grand. You can meet her there," and Lyle said, "All right," not even thinking of the fact that he'd owned no car in five years, and he followed as they carried the stretcher down the stairs and out the door. On the sidewalk they extended the legs of the stretcher and rolled her to the open door of the ambulance, and slid the stretcher in, smoothly efficient.

"Thank you," Lyle said. One of them climbed into the back of the ambulance with her, and, bending beside her, he said, "Right, so—you'll come along to Casualty, then," and then the other said, "They'll get her sorted, I wouldn't worry," and closed the door. "Thank you," Lyle said again, and stepped back from the ambulance, and they drove away.

Out here in the silent empty street, what lingered was that odd, hushed sociability of men, and this cool air through his pajamas against the skin of his shins and back. Standing here in his thin, worn slippers, some part of him imagined

driving, not the last car he'd had, the sensible small sedan
men like him drove in America, but the first car, the 1941
Mercury he'd bought when he was eighteen, in 1950. He
could feel, for a moment, the easy play of the big steering
wheel, the soft bounce of the broad front seat, the breeze
through the vent window, and how high off the road he'd
been, how these Galway streets would roll low and smooth
before him.

The cool air moved, and brushed the leaves of a hedge,
and then, from far off, came the sound of some real car,
and then at the edge of his vision a light came on in the
back of a house across the street. The world re-created
itself around him. He was standing in the street. He had to
dress and call a cab and go. And he wouldn't be driving a
narrow road in Vermont, with his youth and confidence
and hope as bright as the spots of sun shifting and glowing
beside him on the maroon seat of that old Mercury. He'd
be riding, in the backseat of a small Irish taxi, in the dark,
to the hospital.

He turned and walked through the gate and turned to
close it, and turned again to the front door of the house, and
there lay Lady, just past the threshold, her muzzle on her
crossed front paws, her sad eyes meeting his.

He nodded to her, and she sighed.

Where had she been through all this? Not underfoot, that
he could recall, not barking.

"We had a little excitement, didn't we," he said. "Didn't scare you, did it?"

She sat up then, alert to the question in his voice, and he went to her and touched her small, sleek head. "I tell you what," he said. "I may be gone for a while, so let's get you outside for a few minutes."

She turned and led him through the house to the back door and stood waiting. He checked his watch—2:40—and realized he didn't know when he'd called 999 or how long he'd stood in the street. He opened the back door, and Lady glanced up at him. "Go on," he said, and the little dog trotted obediently out into the backyard. "I have to make a phone call—I'll leave the door open," he said after her.

Then things went quickly: he called the taxi, Lady came in and he gave her her treat and put her in her crate in the laundry room with her toy, and he was dressed and had written Róisín's phone number on a slip of paper before he heard the taxi outside. No need to call her until morning, he was sure, no point in calling until he'd heard what the doctors said. He checked that he had his wallet and keys, and went again out the front door and into the street, where the first light made the trees pale and the taxi waited.

Lyle got in, and told the cabbie, "University Hospital—Casualty."

"Is it for yourself?" the cabbie asked, pulling smoothly away from the curb.

"No," Lyle said. He had no wish to say more, but when the man didn't ask, he began to feel it was rude not to. "My wife."

"Sorry to hear it," the cabbie said, and then, as he took the next corner, "They're good there at University, the doctors."

"So I've heard."

"My sister's husband was in hospital there last year. He had gallstones. They did right by him."

"Good to know," Lyle said, and then they were both quiet until the hospital was in sight, and Lyle said, "Easy driving this time of day."

"It is that," the man said. "Nobody else out."

"You drive every night?"

"Just the three nights."

And then they took the turn into the hospital and stopped in front of the lighted door, and there was nothing more to say except "How much is it?" and "Two pounds" and "Thank you" and "Good luck to you—God bless" and "Thanks again," though Lyle now almost desperately wanted to ask the man which three nights, and if he had a wife, children, was he from Galway, how many years had he been a cabbie, anything to keep from having to walk, as he now did, through the door, anything to keep from having to speak to the woman in the glassed-in cubicle.

The woman nodded when he said Mary's name, said ambulance, said husband, and she looked down at papers and then said, "She's in the Resuscitation Room just now, Mr. Sullivan. If you'll take a seat just there, the doctor will find you."

So Lyle took a seat in the empty waiting room, and waited, and did not think about resuscitation. After a long empty time, a young woman doctor appeared behind the woman in the cubicle, spoke to her, the woman pointed to Lyle, and the doctor came out and shook his hand.

They say it's pneumonia," Lyle said.

"It is of course," Róisín said, shaking the rain from her umbrella. The hospital corridor was narrow and noisy, and smelled of toast. "She always had the weak chest."

The surge of irritation that rose into Lyle's throat—he'd lived with Mary for almost forty years, knew her far better than her sister did, and had never known her to have a weak chest—was almost welcome, the first ordinary thing he'd felt in the hours since Mary fell.

"Well, she's got it now," he said.

Róisín had gotten her umbrella furled and snapped, and she turned to start down the hallway. "She's in St. Mary's ward, is she?" she said almost over her shoulder.

It gave Lyle a small pleasure to say she was wrong. "No. She's in the ICU," he said, and that small pleasure dissolved completely as he heard his voice actually say "ICU," and saw the honest alarm in Róisín's quick turn back to him, although her face slid almost immediately into a skeptical half frown.

"Intensive care for pneumonia?" she said.

"For a while, they said. Her temperature's not coming down as fast as they'd like."

"Can we see her?"

"The nurse said I could come back about nine."

Róisín tapped the point of her umbrella on the floor and seemed to tell the time from the pattern of small, bright drops that danced from it. "We'll have a cup of tea, then, in the canteen, and you can tell me about it," she said. She looked up and met Lyle's eyes fully for the first time—for a swift second it seemed to him it was the first time ever—and nodded. "You look like you could use a cup—you're a sight."

For Lyle that first day went on as if he were only an observer: doctors came, Róisín said things, nurses checked things and adjusted things, Mary coughed or seemed to sleep uneasily, he drank tea he didn't want from cardboard cups and went and stood beside her bed for long blank periods between visits by one or another of the doctors. Everyone was cheerful, everyone was polite, and he had no idea what he ought to do. Late that first afternoon, Róisín told him to go home, tend to the dog and take a shower, or, better, she said, he should have a good rest: "You had no sleep, did you? Go on so—I can stay. I'll ring Norah to step in and get Michael his tea."

So Lyle went home, unlocked his kitchen door, and opened it into a wide silence.

This had happened before.

One afternoon in the October when he was nine, when he lived with his widowed mother in a four-room, ground-floor apartment in Bellows Falls, Vermont, and spent Saturdays with his grandmother because his mother worked in a laundry, the weather had turned unexpectedly cold, and his grandmother had sent him home for a sweater. That day he had stepped, this way, into the kitchen, and had felt the home he knew expand around him. Then, too, the kitchen floor had seemed remarkably clean and continuous, and had seemed, as this floor now did, to signal that important things had been hidden from him until now. He had felt free and illicit, almost weightless, standing then, as now, with his hand still on the doorknob, as if he might, in a kind of clicking invisibility, walk into any room and see into some new knowledge, of his mother, of his life.

Now, although he didn't recall that day, didn't even register that it was the seductive tentativeness of a memory that made him turn his head, as if listening for something, Lyle stopped in the doorway of this house in Ireland, and felt the ghost of that temptation, that promise of revelation. If the dog had not made her one glad bark of welcome, he might have walked through the rooms he and Mary had shared for the past five years as he had, long ago, walked through his mother's rooms, touching things, disappointment growing to irritation and then sullenness. Walking back to his grandmother's he had whispered swearwords, as if the errand had been onerous, unfair, unkind.

But Lady did bark, and Lyle called out to her, "Hello, girl," and took her leash from the hook beside the door.

By the time he'd walked with her to the prom and back, an abbreviation of their routine, he was exhausted, the lost night's sleep and the day's static worry insisting. Upstairs, the remnants of the night's drama had become only disorder: he moved the rocker back into the guest room, folded the blanket and laid it across the foot of the bed, crossed the hall to their bedroom, and lay down and slept, deep and dreamless, as he had slept (although he didn't remember it, as he wouldn't remember this) almost thirty years ago, the night after Jimmy was born, the last time Mary had left him for a whole night in their bed on his own. The telephone rang at ten. He knew he must have waked, because he remembered seeing the clock, and he must have spoken coherently, but Róisín's voice—"They're after moving her into the ward now," she said, "so I'd say she's improving. I've come home, and you might get a night's sleep. There's no need of us sitting up in the waiting room like tinkers"— seemed still to hang in the air when he came fully awake at dawn, famished, the dog a warmth against his back.

They were nearly out of butter.

Clean towels were in the dryer; she hadn't had the energy to hang them outside, or last night to fold them and put them in the press, but they were clean and dry.

"They moved her back here in the night."

"Is it for the oxygen?" Róisín said.

"It's a ventilator," the nurse said.

"Ah."

"To help her breathe."

She must tell him the two pounds beside the telephone were for the Salt Hill lotto, and the little girl Audrey would call by for it today on her way to her piano lesson, and he mustn't tease her or try to joke—she was a timid bit of a girl and would be frightened enough that it was Lyle instead of Mary opening the door to her.

"So she's very bad."

"They're using a different antibiotic," Lyle said.

"A different one? You saw the doctor, did you, so early?"

When Mary became aware of voices beyond a mesh of sounds mechanical and oceanic, the listing in her mind of things to tell Lyle seemed to have been going on without her

for a long time, and she lay listening, as if the reminders
were not her own.

She'd left Lyle on his own only once except when the boys
were born, and she'd come home that time after three weeks
to a nearly empty refrigerator and him using the same towel
and sleeping in the same sheets since she'd been gone, and
every stitch he owned in a heap beside the washing machine.
He didn't know where she kept the washing powder, he'd
said, but she knew better: he didn't know how, didn't know
what needed to be done (there was the toilet unscrubbed all
that time, and Prince drinking from it day and night, potatoes gone to soup in the bag, the paperboy three weeks in
arrears)—oh, she'd had to go away then in such a rush, her
father taken so bad, no time to prepare him or leave instruc-
tions, just like this!

"I talked with her in the hall."

"Did you have breakfast at all?"

"A little. Enough."

When she'd had to go into hospital to have the boys, she'd
had her friend Joan come in each day, Joan O'Brien who had
been a nun, and she'd kept everything right, and come again
and helped after Mary and the baby came home.

"She always had a weak chest."

"Did she?"

"Maybe we should just let her rest."

"Are you sleeping, Mary?"

There was something else about a baby, a baby she'd heard crying, but she was too weary to remember. She let it go, but must remember to tell him not to chance that chicken salad in the yellow dish on the left, behind the cheese: it had gone off for sure by now, and she'd meant to throw it away and had only forgotten. The dog was to have her oil capsule today, but Thursday would do as well, just once a week. He might want to call round to the Fannings before the weekend and see if they still wanted the loan of the punch bowl.

"It's best to let her rest while she can."

"It is of course. I only wondered could she hear us."

"I'd say she can."

"You'll be fine in a day or two, Mary—I'll take care of this fellow for you."

The coughing returned, took its time, and passed. Someone—oh, it was doctors, she knew that, she knew that well enough—did something to her arm, something to her head, and then that was over, and she waited then to see what else her memory would send up.

The card for Nancy MacAuliffe, that used to be Long, for her new baby girl named Róisín, was beside the phone, too, all stamped and addressed, if he'd just drop it in the post. Did he not remember Nancy, who went for a doctor and married John MacAuliffe, that nice poetry fellow?

No, he wouldn't remember that. So much he forgot, or

never knew. The size of her was one: Christmas he'd given her a small nightgown and a giant skirt, God love him. The size of himself, for all that, he hadn't a clue, she knew that, hadn't bought himself a scrap of clothing in more than thirty years that she knew of.

"A word with you, if I may."

"Sure."

She'd kept the nightgown, though, thinking of her granny growing so suddenly tiny when she was sick, and how sad the old men looked shrunken inside the collars of their old shirts. He should think of that, and buy the new shirts that fit, not just the size of the old ones.

The morning nurses were just coming on duty when the consultant of the team assigned to Mary put his hand on Lyle's shoulder and nodded to Róisín and said, "A word with you, if I may." He was a slender man, soft-spoken, from Donegal, Róisín had said, and Lyle had thought Mary would like him, when she woke up; she'd admire his curly hair and say appreciative things about his delicacy, his patience, his sad eyes. His eyes were sad now, as he explained about this particular kind of pneumonia, gesturing with his graceful hands, about the varied and increasing resistance of staphylococcus bacteria, about white-blood-cell counts, about the limits of medicine, the power of the will, the mysteries.

When he was gone and Róisín and Lyle stood in the corridor, Róisín hissed.

The sound startled Lyle, and he turned and looked at her, and saw the furious pallor of her face.

"What?" he said.

She shook her head, closed her eyes for a second, and pressed two fingers hard to the center of her forehead, a gesture so familiar that Lyle suddenly didn't know what Mary's face looked like. He turned from Róisín and hurried into the ward. He was panting, and he forced himself to stop, to draw a single deep breath. He smoothed his hair with the palms of both hands, touched his throat, and approached her bed.

She lay as before, propped on pillows to ease her breathing, the clear mask of the ventilator covering her nose and mouth, the IV taped to her left hand. Someone had brushed her hair back from her forehead, and he saw the awesome fragility of her temples. Then for the first time he knew she was dying.

"Mary?" he said, softly, the first word he had spoken to her since he'd shouted her name in the guest room a hundred years ago.

The machines went on sighing and blipping, and she didn't stir.

"Mary," he said again, meaning *Come back,* and touched the spun lightness of her hair.

Kevin didn't start cutting the chicken into serving-size pieces that Thursday night until after ten o'clock, even though the recipe said it should marinate twenty-four hours and he meant to start cooking it at six the next evening. He had put the marinade together as soon as he arrived home from work, and he could have done the chicken then, but he was working on breaking himself of that kind of fussy precision, so he had put the marinade in the refrigerator and gone out alone for a burger and a movie before coming back to the kitchen. He knew that the recipe's twenty-four hours was very broadly approximate, and he knew, too, that if it didn't turn out perfectly, he'd wonder if the four hours would have made a difference, but he was also just a little bit proud of himself. Rachel, teasing, used to threaten to write a book called *Good Habits That Go Bad and the Men Who Have Them.* He sliced through the tendon at the joint between thigh and drumstick, pleased with the sharpness of the knife, and half considered calling her—they were still friends, in a way, and she liked to stay up late. He could say, What are you up to? And she'd say, Not much, you? And he'd say, Oh, I've just put some chicken in to marinate.

He shook his head and grinned, trimming the fat from the underside of the breast skin. Great conversation, Kev. Then what? Are you going to say, I was supposed to put it in at six, and, hey, I'm just getting around to it now? Right.

On the other hand, she might say, Oh, yeah—who you cooking for? And he could say, Oh, just some people from work, and so she'd know—she always caught such things—that he was finally seeing somebody, and she'd be extra nice. Sisterly.

He used the poultry scissors to cut the breasts in half. And he'd probably make his pitiful boast about the four hours, and she'd laugh and congratulate him, and when he got off the phone, he'd feel like a complete fool. He separated the two blades of the scissors and washed and dried them.

He arranged the chicken pieces in the glass dish and told himself he should be thinking about Kathy, not Rachel, since she was the one who'd be eating the chicken, for crying out loud. Kathy. Kathleen Phelan, from Product Development, the prettiest redheaded woman he'd ever seen, but at this moment he couldn't get past those facts, couldn't find the woman herself in his mind with Rachel's dark hair and smoky voice filling it up.

He rinsed his hands at the sink and then, feeling absurd and rebellious, went ahead and pumped the antibacterial soap onto his palm and lathered up. Without glancing at the dish of chicken, he knew, though he'd put them in without thinking, that the pieces were perfectly—obsessively—alternated and spaced. And that, by God, was how they ought to be. And Kathy—well, the hollow at the base of her throat tasted elusively of peaches—how do you like *that*? He dried his hands and poured the marinade over the chicken. And she had taken him to his first-ever hockey game, and she had an ugly, friendly dog of indeterminate breed. She was afraid of fireworks and hookworm. He covered the chicken and slid it into the refrigerator, rinsed out the marinade bowl and put it into the dishwasher. And she had a Ph.D. in literature and she shaved her goddamned legs.

He ran both hands along the sides of his head and lifted his chin and, with his right hand, smoothed his throat in two quick passes. The only thing dumber than calling your old girlfriend, he thought, was insulting her when she wasn't even there, but still, when the phone rang after he'd gotten into bed, something just above his diaphragm did leap with something like hope that it might be Rachel.

Jimmy set the pitcher at an angle under the tap, pulled it on, scooped ice into two glasses, and poured the shots for two gin and tonics while the pitcher filled. It was a good night, steady, loud but not noisy, and he was keeping up and a little ahead without breaking a sweat. At the other end of the bar, Shirley was cracking jokes with the five out-of-town businessmen who'd been there since happy hour. Shirley Stephens was a pro, easily the best bartender Jimmy had ever worked with, and he paid attention, as he made change and took an order for three margaritas and a club soda with lime. She was fast and efficient behind the bar, but she was doing something else, too: she was slowing these guys down, subtly, keeping them happy and together and under control while she covered the rest of her half of the long bar. The five men were staying in the motel across the parking lot, so it wasn't a driving issue, but in half an hour, when the pace picked up before last call, you didn't want one of them getting chummy with a local girl, mistaking signals the way a guy sometimes did after seven or eight hours in a bar, and getting himself into a jackpot with a boyfriend or husband. In half an hour, you wanted each of the five of them to believe that Shirley was the redheaded girl of his dreams, and then they'd sit tight until closing, and then—then Jimmy would cheerfully move them out with the rest of the crowd, and they'd shake their heads and grin kind of sheepishly and shuffle back to their rooms, and hit the road tomorrow, head back to their wives or whatever and Shirley would go home to her husband, Herb.

He liked tending bar because it was that kind of complicated. There were the regulars, people like Harold and Greg who never caused any trouble, or like Brady and Mike who might cause a little excitement but no real trouble, and the sporadic locals, like Peterson and Bennett, who were regulars elsewhere and could be trouble here, depending. There were the one-day-a-week people, like Kenny Collins, who came through the door just then and gave Jimmy a wave, and like Dr. Molino, who came in every Sunday at exactly three o'clock, had exactly two very dry martinis, and tipped exactly $1.25. When Kenny got to the bar, he'd order the Rolling Rock that Jimmy had just opened and jammed into the ice bucket, and he'd spend this last hour to closing carrying the beer around, talking to everybody; Jimmy had never seen him actually drink from the bottle. These were men with real lives, and this place, The Oaks, was a small but important part of those lives, and Jimmy liked being part of the team that kept The Oaks profitable and, at the same time, a place such people were happy to come. Okay: he was proud of this work, especially on nights like this, when everything swung along and you could watch how it was supposed to be.

He took another order, pitcher and four glasses, pointed his finger at the next person as he started the pitcher, two gin and tonics, no fruit. Three couples, dressed up, an after-dinner group, came through the door laughing. The phone rang, and he glanced down the bar—Shirley had it. He poured the gin. It was almost one, and in a couple minutes the pace would pick up, last call coming on, the sprint:

Jimmy loved the sprint on a night like this, mild outdoors, the door open to let the air in and the smoke out, everybody with a little spring fever, a little sunburn across the nose, busy but mellow.

"Hey, Sully—phone!" Shirley called from the other end of the bar. Jimmy nodded, grabbed the phone from the wall at his end, and tucked it on his shoulder so his hands were free, set the glasses for the pitcher on the bar. "Hello," he said into the phone.

"Jim. It's Dad."

Jimmy topped off the pitcher. "Dad?" He took the ten-dollar bill from the girl and turned to the cash register.

He almost said, Dad Who? He almost said, Whose dad?

"Have you got a pencil?"

"Have I got a pencil?" He counted the girl's change into her palm, smiled his thanks as she slid a dollar back across the bar. His father had never, never, telephoned him before. "I'm working."

But there was Shirley beside him, a pen and a bar napkin in her hand, and she took over his end of the bar without even looking at him. He turned to the back bar.

"Okay—yeah. I've got a pencil."

"Listen: your mother's very sick. You'll—"

"Dad? What do you mean, very sick?"

"She has pneumonia, she's in the hospital. You'll need to—"

"What hospital?"

"Here in Galway. Write down this number. It's my credit card, and you can get your plane ticket on it."

"Okay. But—"

But his father started reading the number, and he wrote it. "Read it back to me, can you?"

And Jimmy read it back.

"All right," his father said. "She's in University Hospital in Galway, and I'm here, too, so you might as well come right to the hospital. You fly into Shannon, and the bus gets you here about as fast as anything else, and then take a cab—you can get a cash advance on that card, too, if you need it. Let me give you the pin number."

"I've got enough," Jimmy said. "Dad, is she—"

"And listen—there probably won't be a flight until afternoon, so you should have time—go to Corson's and buy a suit."

"A suit. Right."

He hung up the phone and stared at the number.

"Hey, Sully—tap a keg of Killian's, would you?" Shirley said.

"Sure," he said. He tucked the napkin into his shirt pocket, grabbed the key off the back bar and got downstairs and as far as the door of the taproom before his knees buckled.

Michael and Norah are here," Róisín said, "and Barty. Fionnuala will be along."

Lyle nodded, but he watched his own fingers stroking the back of Mary's hand for a long moment before he could stop. "I might go home and see to the dog," he said.

"The priest is here, too."

"She'll want her own priest," Lyle said. Hours earlier Róisín had telephoned Father Cronin, and found he was away for the day, and had brought the hospital priest. Lyle had said then, She'll want her own priest; he'd said it quietly then, and his voice was still quiet and even now.

"What's important is that it's a priest at all," Róisín said.

"There's no hurry," Lyle said. "They said he'll be back by seven." He stood, his eyes still on Mary's quick, steady breathing. "I'll be back in an hour."

Róisín sighed. "Get you something to eat, Lyle—it's half five."

Outside the ICU, Lyle shook hands with Róisín's husband, Michael, and then with their daughter, Norah, who murmured something, and with Barty, her son, who had outgrown the earrings of his adolescence and looked nearly respectable. Lyle nodded to the young priest but walked on without any more greeting. She would want her own priest.

Once he was outside, out of the hospital entirely and in the evening air, he wasn't as certain, either that she'd want her own priest or that there was no hurry, and he had to close his eyes and remember the steadiness of her breathing, the fact of the boys' coming, the newest antibiotic, to keep himself from hurrying back inside. She would want her own priest, and she would wait for the boys, and modern medicine was full of miracles. To prove it, he walked across the car park and then across the busy street to a shop that had a small deli, where he bought a cup of tea and a ham sandwich. He carried them down a block to the canal, where swans floated and the angelus rang from the cathedral as he watched them and ate half the sandwich before he started back to the hospital. He remembered the dog with a lurch of guilt that was near panic as he climbed the stairs back to the ICU.

Barty stood in the corridor, playing some game on his cell phone, and Lyle hurried to him: he would borrow the phone and call Mary, ask her to take the dog out, and feed her.

"Ah, Uncle Lyle," Barty said, "Father Cronin's come— they got him on his mobile."

"Oh," Lyle said, trying to think who Father Cronin was.

Jimmy had gotten his hair cut, the back of his neck trimmed close, with a white line between hair and sunburn like a joint of white bone. That was the first thing Kevin noticed, as if seeing his brother in Newark Airport were the most ordinary thing in the world. Minutes later, when it occurred to him that he ought to have been surprised to see him at all, he explained to himself that it wasn't really remarkable: there were only so many flights to Ireland from so many airports, and it made sense that Jimmy, leaving from Cleveland, would end up in the same place that Kevin did, leaving from Indianapolis. But in this first moment, as Kevin stood in the airport bar watching people pass and saw, a head taller than the others, his brother, what seemed remarkable was the haircut, and the rigid gravity of Jimmy's pace going down the long corridor to their gate. The store logo on the garment bag Jimmy carried over his shoulder—Corson's—was still immediately translatable to Kevin, though he hadn't lived in Cleveland for almost ten years; the haircut and the suit that must be in the bag were both clearly new, purchased in the hours since the telephone call, whereas his own haircut and his own suit were as they had been before. Distantly, like an echo of Rachel's voice, Kevin noticed his own reflexive complacency, and disliked it.

He disliked even more that he let his brother walk by, didn't step away from the bar to intercept him, greet him, embrace him.

He stood there with his hand on his cold beer glass and

hoped that they wouldn't meet until they stepped onto Irish soil.

So he had to sprint to catch up with him, his own garment bag flopping against his back, the taste of the beer sour on the roof of his mouth as he clapped his brother on the shoulder.

"Jimmy," he said, and then they were face to face.

Both faces flickered with the question, Did she die?

"Kevin!"

They shook hands, grinning cautiously, their eyes still asking, Do you know that Mary Sullivan is going to die? They said they were looking good.

"Nice haircut," Kevin said, teasing.

Jimmy made a wry face, shrugged. "Dad said bring a suit," he explained, and then, hearing that said, they both looked away. "I'm in first class on the way over," Jimmy said, almost shyly. "It was all that was left."

"Me, too," Kevin said, and they both wanted to say how expensive it was, but that was a thing they couldn't say now.

"When'd you get in?" Jimmy said.

"A little after three—you?"

"Just now."

"So did you talk to him again?"

Jimmy shook his head. "Not since last night, about midnight."

They both started to shift their garment bags from one shoulder to the other, and both stopped.

"You want to get a beer or something?" Kevin said.

"They'll give us dinner on the plane, right?" Jimmy said.

"Dinner, movie—probably two movies."

"Free drinks, right?"

"You've got a point," Kevin said.

"Besides," Jimmy said, and grinned again, "I worked last night—had about all the bar time I need for a while."

"I hear you," Kevin said, and then disliked himself again for the heartiness of his tone, the false sales-meeting words. "Let's just go on down to the gate, you think?"

"Yeah—I was thinking maybe I'd just sit and read for a while." He patted the shape of a book in his jacket pocket. "I been tearing around all day, you know?"

"Me, too," Kevin said.

"Hey," Jimmy said as they walked, "how's Rachel?"

"She's great," Kevin said. "We don't see much of each other anymore, though."

"Shit—I'm sorry."

"Not the end of the world. Just didn't work out. You seeing anybody?"

"Not for a while now."

In the gate area itself, a moment of silence fell as they were draping their garment bags over one of the seats, and in that

silence they heard an Irish woman's voice, answering someone a few seats away, "Ah, you can of course, God love you."

"Jesus Christ, Kevin," Jimmy said, their fear loose on his
face and in his voice.

The summer Jimmy was six and Kevin was ten, they
played neighborhood baseball every afternoon in Neal
O'Donoghue's backyard and walked home at suppertime
side by side, each with an arm draped around his brother's
neck, skinny, tanned little boys, shirtless in the heat, dust in
the sweat on their bare legs, no more aware of their embrace
than of that dust. By the next summer, they wrestled,
punched each other, and began to shake hands, and by the
next year, when Kevin was twelve, even handshakes disappeared, until they were men.

They gripped one another now, chest to chest, harsh and
involuntary, almost violent, a contact brief and necessary, as
embarrassing as it was comforting.

They parted, awkward, each with a confused sense of his
brother's shoulders and arms, his scent and strength, and
each touched his own face, ran a palm across the jaw, the
chin, and looked away.

"It might not be that bad," Kevin said finally.

Jimmy nodded. "Yeah. We won't know, I guess. Until we
get there."

Kevin sat down. "Long way from here to there," he said.

"Hey," Jimmy said, and he, too, sat down, their suits on

the seat between them, "what do you know about this bus from Shannon to Galway?"

Kevin snorted a laugh. "I know I rented a car, for Christ's sake."

They didn't speak of it again. They didn't compare seat assignments—Kevin was two rows behind Jimmy—and they didn't request to be seated together. Neither of them told the kind and soft-voiced flight attendant the purpose of their journey, although each of them, fleetingly, imagined her intelligent sympathy: she was very pretty, dark-haired, from Ballyduff in Kerry, and her name was Janette, and she had a daughter named Aoife, and both of them would remember her and her name and her daughter's name and the name of her hometown for many years. Neither of them had slept the night before; each of them drank two glasses of wine with dinner, and both of them wandered into sleep as the plane passed over Newfoundland.

The sun was just up when they started the descent into Dublin, and full and bright by the time they landed in Shannon and started the drive to Galway, and still they didn't speak of their mother. They agreed that they thought they knew where the hospital was; they agreed that there was no need to stop, that the breakfast on the plane hadn't been bad at all, that the roads were, as they had been before for each of them on their separate visits over the past four years, still surprisingly narrow. They agreed that it was good that this early in the morning, just past seven because they'd had a good tailwind and their flight had arrived a little ahead of schedule, this early there was almost no traffic. They agreed that the Irish tended to get a later start on their day than Americans.

Neither of them said aloud that their father was vivid to them, standing beside a hospital bed, motionless, his hands hanging.

She should tell Lyle about the new box of washing powder in the hall press.

Jimmy couldn't bear wool on his skin. It was Kevin liked the fig bars, and two pillows on his bed.

Hanging on the hook in the laundry room was a carry bag with a few tins of food he didn't care for and a few other bits and pieces, and the whole bag was for the Traveller woman when she came to the door, usually on a Thursday.

The bit of cheddar that looked so dry was really fine, she'd grate it over something, and no need to waste it. Cheese kept, like drink. They'd have to make certain of enough drink, with so many in the house.

How many? Half Oranmore, Da said, the thirsty half for certain, and he just hoped they'd make some decent music, not those sad old songs. Ah, Mam said, they're good songs, the old ones, and Aunt Norah said they were, they were, her hands turning the bread and turning the bread, but think of it, Maeve, she said, hearing those songs from when you were like these ones on the floor and right enough it must be terrible for them going away to think they'd never hear them again.

Terrible if it's this lot singing them, Da said, a memory like that for all your days, you'd need the priest in to do an exorcism just to get the noise of it out of your head, and who knows what priests they have over there?

A priest is a priest, Mam said, go on with you now, flicking water from her hands at him, it's your own brothers and sisters in it, too.

It's James we're waiting for, is it? Lyle said.

Ah, no, Róisín said, he's gone for a priest this long time, you know that.

If he has committed any sins, they will be forgiven, Lyle said.

Amen, they said.

Such a crowd of them all around, and all Lyle's packing still to be done. She must remember the shirt with the blue stripe, and the blue figured tie that went with it, and he'd need his warmer pajamas, wouldn't he? Or no—it was a fine hotel, he'd said, he'd be too warm in those, so the broadcloth. Just the one set, for the five days. Was it five days? Or was this the longer trip? No matter. And then his shaving things, and she'd not aired the suitcase yet as she'd meant to. With all these people about, it was mad to think of spreading it in the garden for the sun to get at, but how else was it to be done, and him off in the morning at first light. Mind yourself, she'd say to him, as the others came around, no moment then to be saying anything else. She'd said so little, it seemed now—told him so few things, never mentioned how she took pleasure in seeing his head, the shape of it, or how she thought his hands were beautiful, even if he was a man—beautiful hands. And other things: she'd seen his eyes full of tears when the boys were baptized and never said a thing about it, and she'd seen how he would put the newspaper to the side for a long time after he read something sad, about children or poor people, for all that he went on about the politics. She'd never told him that his smell was a joy, a rich wheaten smell that was almost a taste, and that when he was away, she'd take his pillow for her own just to have that smell of him close, and she'd plan then to tell him everything—and then it would seem she needn't tell him a thing, that he knew it all already. But there he was—she heard his voice in the crowd of noise, and she heard the boys, too, come for the party—and he was off in the morning, and she'd tell him this time, she'd find a quiet moment, once she'd finished the packing she'd call him away and tell him, before he went away.

The sons had arrived, people said, in time.

One by one, over the next six hours, her organs failed. The doctors came and went, quietly; Michael and Norah waited in the hall, Fionnuala came and sat with them; the rules for the ICU were bent to allow the four of them, the sister and husband and sons, to stay; the nurses had drawn the curtains around the bed. Just after three in the afternoon of the last day of June, Father Cronin stood with them, and the respirator was turned off, and she was still.

"Saints of God," he said, quietly, "come to her aid! Come to meet her, angels of the Lord!"

And Róisín answered, "Receive her soul and present her to God the Most High."

And the priest: "May Christ, who called you, take you to himself; may angels lead you to Abraham's side."

And the boys remembered and spoke with their aunt, "Receive her soul and present her to God the Most High."

"Give her eternal rest, O Lord, and may your light shine on her forever."

And then Lyle, too, clearing his throat, said with the others, "Receive her soul and present her to God the Most High."

"Let us pray. Father, we entrust our sister to your mercy. You loved her greatly in this life: now that she is freed from all its cares, give her happiness and peace forever. The old order has passed away: welcome her now into paradise, where there will be no more sorrow, no more weeping or pain, but only peace and joy with Jesus, your Son, and the Holy Spirit forever and ever."

"Amen."

After a long moment, the priest turned and went out of

the curtained cubicle, and Róisín touched each of the men before she followed him, crying quietly.

They had never expected to find themselves without her. But there, surrounded by the soft light through the curtains, they began to make the choices and decisions that must follow a death. People who had known them for years, who knew the tensions and disappointments, the tempers and failures that joined and separated these three men, would have urged Róisín to remain with them, to keep peace as her sister had done for so long. People who knew any one of them—Lyle with his disgruntlements, Kevin with his finickinesses, Jimmy with his irresponsibilities—would have scoffed at the idea of them there, in this odd peace, beginning to speak of music she had loved, people to be called, necessary arrangements to be made. But those people weren't there, in that first hour. There was no one and nothing to disturb them, to insist that they were other than Mary had always hoped them to be, and so, in that hour and in the hours that remained of that day and in the decisions and then the rituals that followed those decisions, they acted as she knew they could, appropriately and well.

❧

If Mary had been there, she would have said, You're never off down the prom in those shoes, are you? and Lyle would have said back that it made no difference to him, but if it would make her feel better, he'd change.

But she wasn't there, and so at eight o'clock in the evening of the day of her funeral, he was walking slowly home from the bay, still wearing his dark suit, his tie still tied, his feet throbbing. Half the world, it seemed, had come to Róisín's house after the burial, and he'd spent almost five hours sipping tepid tea and eating sandwiches that tasted like so much cardboard, listening to dozens of people he didn't quite recognize tell him what a wonderful woman his wife had been, what handsome men his sons were, what a lovely service it had been. The day had been hot and was still sunny when he set out at a little after six, leaving Kevin and Jimmy at the house: he was determined to give Lady a decent walk, determined, too, to be away from everybody. But, of course, the sun had brought everybody else out, and the sidewalks and the beach had been crowded with tourists and baby strollers and running children and unleashed dogs. Beautiful, he supposed, but too damned hot to be out walk-

ing in a suit, and now his shirt was stuck to him and his forehead was tender, so he'd probably gotten burned as well.
And his feet were killing him.

As they walked around to the back door, even Lady was
slow. He unlocked the door and went into the kitchen, bent
to unfasten her leash, and asked her, "Your feet hurt you?"

"Not anymore."

There they were, two of them in the kitchen doorway,
wearing jeans and T-shirts.

"I was talking to the dog," Lyle said.

"Have a good walk?"

"Hot," Lyle said, and sat down on a chair beside the
kitchen table and took Lady on his lap. She licked his chin.
"Over," he told her, and turned her onto her back and ran
his hands up her forelegs to the neat black pads of her feet.
"Hold still," he said, but his hands were shaking, his knees
beneath her shaking. He felt his sons exchange a glance.

He hadn't known who they were.

He hadn't been startled, thinking they'd be out, or somewhere else in the house; he hadn't been surprised, distracted
by the dog. No: *Not anymore,* a barefoot young man slouch-
ing in the kitchen doorway, and the full-body shock of
adrenaline—a lifetime waiting for this to happen, the peace-
ful return to invasion by strangers, the casual menace of
Have a good walk? and immediately the nausea, knowing
his age, their youth, the two of them and one of him, the

clutter of furniture barring flight, the vulnerability of his stoop to unfasten the leash, the pitiable smallness and trustingness of the dog herself.

He pressed a thumb gently against each pad of her feet. She didn't seem to mind.

"You okay?" Kevin said.

"She's fine," Lyle said, and said to her, "Down," and she righted herself and went in her tidy way to the floor and then to Jimmy, who squatted to pet her. "Streets were hot. I thought she might have hurt a foot." He rubbed his hands on his thighs, as if there might be dog hairs to remove from the dark fabric, trying to hide his body's tremor. "She gets a treat now," he said.

"Where are they?" Jimmy said.

"That cupboard," Lyle said, and jerked his head instead of pointing. He could feel the wateriness of every joint in his body. "On the right," he said when Jimmy opened the wrong door.

"You sure you're okay?" Kevin said. "You look like you might have gotten a little sunburn."

"Maybe so," he said. "I'm fine."

"If you had some aloe—"

"I think I'll survive it," Lyle said. All at once he slept, straight in the kitchen chair. When he opened his eyes, Jimmy was grinning, standing in the doorway again, with the telephone receiver held against his heart.

"Aunt Róisín," he said. "She wants to know if she should bring us the leftover sandwiches."

Lyle shook his head no. Kevin came around from behind him and held out his hand for the phone and Jimmy gave it to him. "Aunt Róisín?" Kevin said. He stepped past Jimmy into the hall, following the cord back to the phone table. "That's kind," he said.

Jimmy said, "Are you hungry?"

Lyle shook his head again and stood. He loosened his tie, unbuttoned his collar, took the tie off.

In the hall Kevin was saying, "None of us can, none of us can."

"Do you have any lawn chairs?" Jimmy said.

"No, we don't," Lyle said, puzzled that this was true. A night like this in Ohio, they'd have sat out in the yard, Jimmy was right. "We don't."

Lady trotted back from the hall, and Jimmy bent and touched her head, but she passed him and came to stand beside Lyle.

"Are you hungry?" Lyle said. "Jim?"

"God, no," laughter in his voice. "No way—maybe never again."

"Take care," Kevin said in the hall. "You, too. Good-bye."

Lyle looked at the tie in his hand. It was dark blue with tiny silver dots; he had bought it at Corson's in Cleveland, for his retirement dinner.

Jimmy said, "Get the funeral meats disposed of?"

"Jim," Kevin said, soft but reproving, cautious.

Lyle was swiftly as shy of these two young men as he'd been of the men at that retirement dinner, men he'd worked with for more than thirty years, strange to him at the candlelit tables of the restaurant, strange as these sons of his were to him here in the dusky kitchen. He turned from them and switched on the light over the sink.

"Do you want some whiskey?" he said.

"You've got whiskey?" Jimmy said, and Kevin, still quiet but so quick his word was under Jimmy's, "Jim."

"I do," Lyle said.

"Not for me, thanks," Kevin said.

"Are you having one?" Jimmy said.

The sky was still not dark, and Lyle's reflection in the window over the sink was dim. He watched himself shake his head. "I don't think so," he said, "but you're welcome to it." He tapped the door of the cupboard beside his head. "Top shelf," he said, still looking for the invisible eyes of his reflected face.

"I guess I'll pass, too," Jimmy said.

Lyle nodded, and looked again at his blue-and-silver tie, and smoothed it over the back of his hand. It was damp where it had been against his neck. Like stars far off, the silver dots. "No," he said, "I think I'll just go on up to bed."

He turned to them but looked past them, into the darker hall. "Do you have everything you need?"

"We're fine," Kevin said, and Jimmy said, "We're all set."

It was ridiculous to be so awkward—they'd slept here the last two nights in the beds Róisín had made up for them, Kevin in the guest room and Jimmy on the sleeper couch in the sitting room. "Good," he said. "Then I'll see you in the morning. Just put Lady into the crate before you go to bed— you don't have to latch it, but she likes to sleep in there."

"Right," one of them said, and the other said, "All right," and then he was past them and at the foot of the stairs. He was stopped there by the sense of something forgotten, neglected in his urge to be away from them. "Her toy," he said aloud. "That little pink sock thing—make sure it's in the crate."

"Got it," Jimmy said. "Good night."

"Sleep well," Kevin said.

"Good night," Lyle said, chastened, and went steadily up the stairs.

He's not 'out of it,'" Kevin said. He pulled the other chair out from the kitchen table and sat opposite Jimmy, who had the dog on his lap. "He's exhausted—emotionally and physically."

"He," Jimmy said, and spoke each word slow and separate, "is out of it. He offered us whiskey."

Kevin looked away, at the leash hung on a hook beside the back door, and then he shook his head and grinned. "And I almost took it."

Jimmy ruffled the long hair of the dog's ears. "Drinking with Dad—imagine it."

"Rite of passage."

"Graduation night."

Kevin groaned. "Oh, man, don't even mention it! I didn't drink again for three years—and I still can't do rum."

"I don't remember you being sick. I just remember the Hail Marys."

"Not just them—the whole rosary. Every night for three weeks."

Lady jumped down and trotted away to the laundry room.

"He probably doesn't even know the rosary."

"Oh, it wasn't him—that was all Mom. He just said, 'Moderation in all things, Kevin.'"

Their laughter flared and then sputtered between them, like candlelight there at their parents' table. Lady came back, her limp pink toy in her mouth, and stood eyeing them.

"She's got a present for you," Kevin said.

"Maybe it's for you."

"Nah—she likes you best."

"Call her."

"Hey, I'm not going to try to influence her."

"Can't tell if you don't try."

"I've tried, believe me—every time I've been here."

Jimmy put his hand down, and Lady came and delicately deposited the toy in his palm. "Maybe she's reserving judgment."

"Maybe."

"Are you wisely reserving judgment, Lady?"

She sat.

"He's attached to her," Kevin said. "That's something."

"A very fine something." Jimmy offered the toy back to the dog, and she took it to the doorway and lay down with her chin resting on it. "What do you think he's going to do?"

Kevin shrugged. "He ought to be able to get a good price for the house—Galway's growing like mad."

"So you think he'll come home." He turned, and they sat facing each other now, their hands—Jimmy's longer, Kevin's broader, both with their father's nails—easy on the table.

"Probably. I don't know why he'd stay here."

"Maybe he'll get married again." He met Kevin's eyes. "In a couple of years."

Kevin looked away. "Why not? The world's full of widows—he should be a hot commodity."

"No—seriously. What is he, sixty-six?"

"Seventy. Seventy-one this winter."

"Okay, so he's seventy. He lives a clean life, no bad habits—"

"The whiskey," Kevin said.

But Jimmy didn't smile. "Mom didn't mind him keeping a bottle of whiskey."

Kevin rubbed his jaw with the heel of his hand. "The thing is," he said, "one of us should be married by now—wife, kid, house, room for Gramps."

"You first," Jimmy said. "You're the oldest."

They both smiled then.

"You think he's okay?" Kevin said.

"He's emotionally and physically exhausted," Jimmy said.

"Yeah," Kevin said, and bounced his fist lightly off the back of Jimmy's hand. "So am I."

"What time is it at home?"

Kevin checked his watch. "About four in the afternoon."

"Weird. Almost time for work."

"Time for bed," Kevin said, "for me."

"You go to bed at four in the afternoon?"

"Hey—every chance I get." Kevin pushed his chair back and stood and stretched.

"Sleep tight," Jimmy said.

"Hey, Jim?"

"Yeah?"

"He didn't recognize us, did he? When he walked in?"

Jimmy shrugged. "We're strange-looking guys, you know

that." He stood, too, as if Kevin were a guest to be accompanied to the door, and they walked the three steps across the kitchen together. "He's fine. Ah, lad, there's not a bother on it—he's grand so."

"Don't," Kevin said.

"You're not the boss of me," Jimmy said, and this time their hug was easy, hidden within the pretense of a slow scuffle, headlocks half feinted and repelled, soft slaps to the ear attempted and averted, their arms almost graceful, almost languorous.

The sound of Kevin coming up the stairs, although he didn't in that first moment think of Kevin but only noticed the sound of someone walking carefully, trying not to disturb him, reminded Lyle to bend, finally, from where he sat on the edge of the bed and untie and unlace his shoes. He knew it wasn't Mary coming: there was no danger he'd forget that she was dead. He had seen her die, watched from that first collapse, watched for hours as the mist appeared and faded on the respirator mask, as her coughing stopped and her breathing grew loud; he had seen her grow golden with jaundice when her liver failed, glow there in the hours before, finally, it was over. It had all happened in a murmur, like a conversation overheard at a distance, through walls, but it had happened, he had seen it, the moment the life went away and Mary was gone, leaving a corpse, shrunken, uninhabited. He had stood with his sons in the funeral home beside the body of his wife, and people he hardly knew had come and seen that body, those sons, his own face.

He eased his shoes off: the relief was enormous, and passed immediately. So: Kevin had come up to bed. The two of them had talked for a while down there; he had heard their quiet voices but not what they'd said. And when he'd come in from walking the dog he hadn't known who they were.

He stood in his sock feet and slipped his jacket off. It was still damp, and he put it on the hanger and hooked it to the outside of the wardrobe. The suit would have to be cleaned before he could wear it again. His shirt was damp, too. He unbuttoned it, listening to water running in the other bathroom. He knew that he had been about to say something— that two extra people would use an awful lot of hot water, or that he'd let the shirt dry before he put it in the hamper, or that Róisín's shoulder didn't seem to be bothering her much these days—and that there was no one to say it to. Dully, he knew that this would happen again and again: without forgetting her death, he would overlook her absence, as if, really, the death had had nothing to do with her, or with him.

Still, when it happened, when he'd finished shaving the next morning and noticed himself hoping she hadn't scrambled all the eggs just because the boys preferred them to fried, and understood that the smell of rashers and coffee had tricked him into assuming her presence, the pain was not dull. Her robe and nightgown hung there on the back of the bathroom door, and he couldn't move, could hardly breathe. He hadn't known it would be like this, loss as physical as lust, as complete and as shameless: he groaned aloud and wrenched the door open with such violence that he almost staggered.

But he was breathing again and moving, out of the bathroom and through the bedroom and into the hall where the smell of breakfast was joined by the voices of his sons.

With his hand on the banister he remembered that he'd thought they were burglars last night, and here he was again, about to shout down the stairs, Get out!

He turned and held the wall and walked himself back into the bedroom and shut the door. He sat on the side of the bed and looked at his hands dangling between his knees, shaking there as he panted. "You're going nuts," he whispered to them. "What the hell's wrong with you?" He took two deep breaths. "For crying out loud," he whispered. "Get a goddamned grip on yourself." He squeezed his hands into fists and then stretched the fingers out hard. "You just get a grip. You get yourself down those stairs and you eat that breakfast." He waited for his body to stand, and in a moment his hands moved to his knees and he did stand. "You just get a grip," he whispered again, and he went again into the hall and this time down the stairs and into the kitchen, where Kevin was at the stove dishing scrambled eggs onto a plate and Jimmy sat at the table with Lady on his lap. All three of them turned their heads and looked at Lyle, but it was Lady's eyes he met, and she looked guiltily away and got down.

"Morning," the boys said.

"She's not allowed at the table," he said to Jimmy, and to Kevin, "Hope those eggs are for you." He sat down at his place, only a little more quickly than he'd meant to. The coffee thermos sat on the table.

"You don't want eggs?" Kevin said.

"I don't want scrambled eggs," he said. "Did anybody let the dog out?"

"Yeah," Jimmy said.

"You might want to wash your hands before you eat,"

Lyle said. "She's clean, but she's still a dog." He twisted the thermos top and pumped coffee into his cup.

Kevin brought a plate of sausages and rashers and another of toast to the table. "How do you want your eggs," he said.

"Over easy," Lyle said. He was fine; he was just fine, and in a moment he'd be able to eat, he was sure.

Jimmy stood up—he'd turned out tall, to everybody's surprise; he'd been such a small kid—and went to the kitchen sink and turned on the water.

"Did you boys sleep well?" He stirred sugar into his coffee.

"Fine," Kevin said. "You?"

"Fine." He took a piece of toast. "Was there any of that blackberry jam in the refrigerator?"

The question hung in the air. Jimmy turned the water off and crossed to the refrigerator where the hand towel hung. He dried his hands before he said, "I'll see," and opened the refrigerator.

Kevin carried the frying pan to the table and lifted the two fried eggs onto Lyle's plate.

"Thanks," he said, and took two rashers and a sausage. "Looks good," he said. Jimmy brought the jam, and both of them sat down. "So do you boys have plans for today?"

"Aunt Róisín called while you were in the shower," Kevin said.

Lyle shook his head. "Didn't she get rid of those sand-wiches yet?"

Again the question hung for a second, and then laughter took both of them.

"Don't choke," Lyle said, though he'd meant to say, Don't laugh with your mouth full, and he spread jam on a bit of toast and ate it. It tasted like toast, like blackberry jam, and then he dared sip the coffee.

"Ahh," Kevin said, and wiped his eyes with the back of his hand. "Hooh. Though to be fair, those sandwiches were sounding pretty good when I woke up at four in the morn-ing." He salted his eggs.

"You've been up since four?" Lyle said.

Kevin shook his head. "I found a banana," he said, so earnestly that Lyle had to chuckle, and then both of them were off again, and Lyle ate most of an egg before they calmed down enough for Kevin to say, "No—anyway, I was hungry, I ate, I went back to sleep. I got up again about eight and went to the store." He gestured to the food on the table.

"I'll pay you for it," Lyle said.

"No way," Kevin said. "My treat, for crying out loud."

For a moment nothing was said, and the sound of silver-ware against plates and cups was loud.

"So what did Róisín want."

"Oh—well, Fionnuala wants us to come to supper to-night."

Jimmy said, "Aunt Róisín doesn't believe Kevin can cook. They think we'll starve."

"I told her I'd check with you and get back to her."

Lyle shrugged. "I don't mind." He liked Fionnuala. She was a niece of Róisín's husband, sensible and quite pretty, and her sons were well behaved.

"So I'll call her and tell her okay."

Lyle wiped his mouth. "All right with me. She lives out the Tuam Road, I think," he warned.

"I think I can find it," Kevin said.

"Aunt Róisín offered to have Barty drive us."

Lyle shook his head, and stood up from the table. "I'll take my chances with Kevin," he said.

"What are you going to do now?" Kevin said.

"Walk along the bay," Lyle said, "like I do every morning, and get the paper." He went to the back door and took his jacket from the peg there, and Lady came trotting to him.

"I got a paper," Kevin said.

"Good," Lyle said, "then we won't have to share one." He was aware of them trading a look as he took the leash from its hook and clipped it to Lady's collar. At least they knew he knew who they were, and if they were giving each other looks, they weren't looking at him.

"You want company?" Jimmy said.

Oddly, surprisingly, he did, though he felt fine now, his breakfast sitting well, the shaking completely gone. "Suit yourself," he said.

Jimmy rubbed his hand over his jaw. "Suppose I should shave," he said.

Lyle looked at him. "You're all right."

Jimmy met his eyes and then grinned. "But I should probably put my shoes on, huh?"

Lyle looked away, out the window, and then he smiled, too. "Probably," he said. "And if you've got a jacket—looks like we'll get rain."

"Surprise, surprise," Jimmy said, but he was up and heading into the living room, where his things were. "I'll just be a sec," he said.

"I brought a slicker if you need it," Kevin called after him.

"I'm cool," Jimmy called back.

Kevin scraped plates.

"It was a good breakfast," Lyle said.

Kevin smiled at him. "Sorry about the eggs."

Lady panted, as close as she ever came to expressing impatience. "I'll be out back," Lyle called into the living room.

"I'm there," Jimmy called back.

The sky was cloudy but the air still warm, and the clouds thinned a little as Lyle stood waiting, so there was actually hazy sunshine on the flower beds in the corners of the yard by the time Jimmy joined him.

"I was going to tell you," he said, "I like the flowers out here—did you plant all this stuff?"

"You've seen it before," Lyle said. He turned away from the garden, and Jimmy followed him down the walk that went around to the gate at the front.

"Nope," Jimmy said behind him. "I was never here in summer before. So is it, like, themes? I mean, with the blue in one corner and the yellow in the other?"

Lyle nodded, and they paused at the gate. "I suppose you did quite a bit of that sort of thing."

"Me?" His jacket was green and light, and if it rained, he'd be drenched.

"With that landscaping job you had."

Jimmy laughed. "I mowed lawns." He turned and looked back at the yard. "I like gardens, though. This new apartment I'm in, there's a place I can plant stuff. I thought I would, next year, if I stay there. What's in that corner?"

"That was going to be all red."

"That'll be nice."

"I've changed my mind," Lyle said, and opened the gate.

"It would look good, though, with the blue and the yellow—now, the marigolds," they went through the gate onto the sidewalk, "now, are those to keep the bugs out?"

Lyle shut and fastened the gate. "No," he said. They were side by side now, walking up the little rise in the street; from the top they'd be able to see the bay. "She just liked them." It wasn't bad, saying that. "I usually walk about five miles in the mornings."

"Sounds good."

They walked on, and when the bay came into sight, Lyle said, "Longest promenade in Europe, they say."

Jimmy nodded, and then they didn't talk anymore until they had crossed the main road to the prom itself, Lady with her ears and tail up. "Gotta love it, huh, girl?" Jimmy said.

"She does," Lyle said. He nodded to another man with a small dog on a leash, and the man nodded back.

"You ever let her just run?" Jimmy said.

"Up there," Lyle said.

Up there was a mile past the Salt Hill roundabout, on a small rocky bit of beach beyond where most of the people who walked the prom stopped and turned back to town. Lyle bent and unclipped the leash. "There you go," he said, and Lady looked him steadily in the eye until he said, "Go on with you," and then she turned and dashed for the water.

"She swims?" Jimmy said.

"Watch."

She charged the small waves, barking, the wind lifting the feathers of her tail and ears, and then she did a miraculous leaping turn and ran back to the rocks as the water followed her. For ten minutes or more, she battled with the bay, and then, her tail high, as if she had won, she trotted sedately back to Lyle.

It wasn't until they were crossing the main road again, heading back to the house that Jimmy said, "Kevin thinks we need to have a talk about the future."

"Your future?"

Jimmy shook his head.

"Kevin worries," Lyle said.

"I was thinking I'd go into town for a while, if that was okay with you."

"You got money?"

"I'm fine."

"Why don't you go on back to the house, then. I'd recommend you get that slicker from Kevin. Tell him I'll be along after I get my paper."

Mrs. Duggan in the shop was taken up with three German women, so he got his paper without having to take condolences with it. When he came out, he saw Jimmy setting off for town, and when he went into the house, he had a moment of hope that Kevin, too, had gone out, but then he heard movement upstairs. He gave Lady her treat, filled her water dish, and took his paper into the living room, only a small part of him preparing to tell Kevin he had no interest in a serious conversation about the future.

But maybe Jimmy had said something to Kevin, warned

him off, because he didn't come downstairs for half an hour, and when he did come down, he brought the other newspaper and sat with it on the couch. Lyle was settled in his chair, catching up on the growing quarrel between the United Nations and George Bush, and when Kevin finally spoke, quite some time later, what he said was, "What do you think about these Palestinians?"

"I think we should have looked before we leapt fifty years ago," Lyle said. "We made the mess."

By then the rain had started, and they read on; after a good while with nothing but the sounds of the pages and the thunder, Kevin said, "I'm going to make a cheese sandwich for lunch—you want one?"

"Sounds good," Lyle said. "There's tea if you want to make a pot." He read a piece about the Real IRA and another about sewage, and then Kevin said, "You want it in there or out here?"

"In here," Lyle said.

The question of the future didn't come up at all until nearly the end of the evening at Fionnuala's. The talk over supper had been about Kevin's work in software and how the software boom in Ireland was collapsing, and then about Fionnuala's own work, the small pottery business she'd started. She wondered if it would be smart to try selling things by mail or on the Internet, to offset fluctuations in the tourist trade, like last year's disaster. They talked about that for a while, how the foot-and-mouth disease crisis had affected travel into the country, and how lucky they'd been that the disease hadn't actually come into the Republic, and then someone asked Jimmy about his work, and the conversation turned to the differences between American bars and Irish pubs, and Róisín told of the pub in Oranmore when she and Mary were growing up there, and how they'd been afraid to pass it. It was the first mention of Mary all night, and Lyle realized he'd been waiting for it, and that, like mentioning her in the morning, it was all right, though he was relieved that the talk turned to the changes in Galway that Jimmy had noticed since the last time he was here. They finished eating, and Jimmy excused himself and went into the sitting room to play a computer game with Fionnuala's young sons. Kevin asked Michael what he thought about the Nice Treaty. Róisín carried plates into the kitchen, and Fionnuala poured Lyle another cup of tea. "Will you be going back, then, Uncle Lyle?" she said.

"Haven't thought about it," he said.

"It's very soon," she agreed. "Do you take sugar?"

If Mary had been there at Fionnuala's, and on the drive home, if she'd been there to go up to bed with him after he'd said good night and left the boys to watch the late news, she'd have said, He fancies her, I'd say, and Lyle would have said, Who?, half sorry he hadn't stayed up for the news himself but so tired he hardly listened to her. Our Jimmy, she'd have said. He fancies Fionnuala.

But she wasn't there and Lyle was that tired. He got into bed and fell immediately into the dreamless sleep her absence opened for him. He didn't remember, as she would have, that Jimmy and Fionnuala had corresponded when they were teenagers, or consider the significance of Jimmy's asking, on the drive home, exactly how Fionnuala was related to them. Lyle slept, and didn't hear even the murmur of the television, or his sons' conversation, how Kevin's voice was so like his own when he said, "Last time I checked, the Fourth of July wasn't an Irish holiday."

"So?" Jimmy said. "Last time I checked, she was self-employed."

"Jim—she's got two kids."

"So? Last time I checked, that wasn't a felony."

And their mother wasn't there to say, Will I make you some tea? so Kevin sighed and said, "You know, when there's a death, people often react—"

"Gee, Kevin, are you saying there's a connection between sex and death? I never thought of such a thing!"

"Okay."

On the television a man talked about an impending strike against a grocery-store chain and the likelihood of Labour Court intervention.

"I'm just saying—"

"What are you saying? Huh, Kev? What?"

"It just doesn't seem the appropriate time."

"Ah."

"Come on—we go back on Friday, for crying out loud—after Dad comes home, there won't be any reason to come here again. Why start something?"

"You talked to him?"

"Well, not yet—"

"Well, I wouldn't start counting on anything."

"Did you talk to him?"

Jimmy shrugged. "He likes his garden. He likes his dog."

"Well," Kevin said, and stood up from their father's chair, "I guess I'll have time to talk to him tomorrow while you're gone."

"I guess you will," Jimmy said.

"Put the dog in her crate tonight."

If their mother had been there, she'd have said, Good night, God bless, and they'd have answered, and the irritation between them would have eased away in the night, and Lyle wouldn't, the next morning, have come downstairs into Kevin's leftover disapproval, when he'd been almost looking forward to Jimmy's company on his walk.

"Where's your brother?" he said. Kevin was at the stove, and there were only two places set at the table.

"He decided to celebrate the Fourth of July by going to

the Aran Islands for the day," Kevin said. He set their plates on the table. "He took Fionnuala and her kids."

Lyle poured his coffee, wary now. "Hope he didn't promise them fireworks."

Kevin snorted.

Lyle ate: the eggs were overdone, but the toast was perfect, just short of burned. Kevin ate, too, stiffly, as if the food offended him.

"This is good," Lyle said.

"Good," Kevin said, and then, "So that's okay with you?"

Lyle shrugged. "Weather's good for it," he said, which, from the way Kevin stood up and started clearing the table, was the wrong thing to say. Lyle held on to his coffee cup and winked at Lady, who sat alert in the doorway. "What are your plans for the day?" he said over the noise of water running into the dishpan.

Kevin turned the water off and stood there with his back to Lyle. "Well, I don't have a date," he said. "I mean, I thought the point was to be together. Now." He put the silverware into the dishpan with a clatter. "Figure things out."

"Plenty of time for that—we've got all day tomorrow," Lyle said. He left the coffee and got his jacket. "No harm in taking a break." He clipped the leash to Lady's collar.

"I suppose," Kevin said, finally. He turned and picked up Lyle's cup from the table. "Have a good walk."

"You want—?"

"No thanks." He put the cups into the dishpan. "Mind if I do some laundry?"

"Fine," Lyle said. "I'll be a couple hours."

Kevin nodded.

"Is he going to be back for supper?"

"About seven-thirty, I think."

"We might go into town," Lyle said. "Go to Scotty's—it won't be too crowded if we go early."

Kevin smiled, a sour smile but a smile. "The Casual American Gourmet—hamburgers big as your head." They'd been there last winter and made fun of the huge portions, the implication of American plenty or American gluttony. Or both.

"American style," Lyle agreed, and let himself out into the cool air.

So they were in Scotty's, downstairs because the street-level room was full, surrounded by signs for American beer and eating American cheeseburgers, when Kevin said, "I don't know how you stand this every summer—wall-to-wall tourists."

"More than summer now—starts up right after Easter, goes through September. They're never all gone, though." He finished his coleslaw. "You just don't go out to eat very often during the season."

"So you're going to cook for yourself now."

Lyle tore off part of his bun and wiped the dressing from the plate and ate the bread, and nodded.

"Come on, Dad—you don't even grill."

"I don't need to grill," Lyle said. He wiped his mouth. "You about done?"

"Listen, I'm not trying to tell you what to do, but how are you going to manage?"

"I'll manage just fine."

"So you're going to stay here."

"Haven't thought about it."

"You guys never talked about it?"

Lyle knew what he should do here: he should explain. He should say, Young man, you don't know a goddamned thing. And he knew, in a swift and embarrassing confusion, that if Mary were here, he would do that—say it, leave the twenty pounds on the table, and walk out—and he knew that because she wasn't here, he couldn't. So he stood up and took his wallet from his pocket, and when Kevin stood, too, in almost the same second, and made a motion toward him, he found himself meeting his son's eyes thinking, Come on, then, big boy—try it.

"Dad," Kevin said, and his hand hovered just above Lyle's forearm, "I'm sorry."

Lyle looked at Kevin's hand, watched it tilt up, palm toward him.

"I was out of line—I'm sorry." The hand went away.

Lyle put the twenty-pound note on the table.

"Okay?"

Lyle nodded, and turned, and they went up the stairs and into the street, where the sun still shone and the sidewalk tables were full; an amplified version of "Whiskey in the Jar" came from somewhere, and three blue-haired young men juggling long sticks blocked the already narrow space left for walking.

"Damned zoo," Lyle said.

"Crazy," Kevin agreed.

Lyle walked straight through the small audience the jugglers had attracted, and he was almost sorry when the jugglers snatched their sticks deftly from the air and stepped back to let him through.

They walked home in silence, and as they came around the corner onto Lyle's block, the last of the sunshine fell on Jimmy sitting in a lawn chair on the sidewalk in front of the gate.

"What the hell," Lyle said.

Jimmy waved, stood, folded the chair, and leaned it against the wall.

"Huh," Kevin said. "He's got more of them."

"Hey," Jimmy said when they got to him.

"What the hell is this," Lyle said.

Jimmy looked at the chairs leaning against the wall. "Chairs."

"On the sidewalk? You waiting for a parade?"

Jimmy shook his head. "I went in the back, but Lady started barking."

"No key," Kevin said.

"Right."

Lyle opened the gate and went around to the back door and let Lady out. The boys brought the chairs around.

"Here okay?" Jimmy said, unfolding the first one.

"Suit yourself," Lyle said. "I'm going in."

"Seems a waste," Jimmy said. He opened the second

chair and sat down and waved his arm at the sky. "Beautiful evening, a nation without mosquitoes, three new lawn chairs."

"Are you drunk?" Kevin said. He unfolded the third chair and stood behind it.

"Only on the charms of the Emerald Isle."

"Give me a break," Kevin said.

"Who knows?" Jimmy said. "There might be fireworks if it ever gets dark." He clasped his hands behind his head.

"It'll get dark," Lyle said. Lady had finished her circuit of the yard and gone to do her business in the far corner. "And there won't be fireworks."

"Come on, Dad, sit out with us awhile. Let me tell you all my adventures. Have you ever been to Inishmore?"

"No," he said. "Come on, girl," he called.

"It's incredible," Jimmy said. "It's like another world—or, no, like the heart of the world. The essence of Ireland."

"Lock up when you come in," Lyle said, and he took the dog inside. They could sit out there and talk about the Aran Islands if they wanted to, or about him if they wanted to do that. He turned off the kitchen light and went into the sitting room, turned on the television.

"Sit down," Jimmy said.

Kevin shook his head, but Jimmy was still looking at the sky.

"So I guess you talked to him," Jimmy said.

"You know, you could help me out a little."

Jimmy stretched his legs out in front of him. "You know, I don't think it's any of my business."

"That's convenient." Kevin folded the third chair back up and stood holding it. "What are you going to do when it's him that gets sick? Have you *ever* paid for your ticket over here?"

In the house, Lyle changed the channel, watched for a moment, and went back to the kitchen. He took down the whiskey and poured himself a small one without turning on the light: no need for them to know every move he made.

"So just what was it that didn't work out with Rachel?"

"I hardly think that's any of your business."

Jimmy hummed a few bars of "Galway Bay."

Lyle took his whiskey back to his chair and sat down and snapped his fingers. Lady came up into his lap, and he tried to watch the show while he sipped the whiskey. It tasted like winter. He closed his eyes and let it be winter—the noise of the wind in the chimney, the whistle of the coal burning— and then he felt ridiculous, and opened his eyes. "Stupid," he said to Lady, and she lifted her head. He pointed with his glass to the two women gabbing on the television. "Ninety percent of it's stupid," he said. He wondered how much he usually talked to the dog. "Might as well go to bed." He finished the whiskey more quickly than he approved of and said, "Get down. You can wait up for them." He left his glass on the table beside his chair and went up the stairs.

"I suppose you're right," Jimmy said.

Kevin leaned the folded chair against the empty one. "Enjoy yourself," he said, and he went inside. The whiskey stood on the counter, and he thought about it for a second, and then put it back in the cupboard, and went up the stairs. They had only one full day left here, and neither Jimmy nor their father seemed to have the least memory of why they were all here together, and clearly they didn't want to be reminded. Well, they could cook their own breakfast tomorrow: he'd get up early and drive to the cemetery.

Tonight sleep came slow for Lyle, his mind crowded at first with things he hadn't said: What do you want me to do—move in with you? Move to Florida with the rest of them? Where the hell do you expect me to store those damned chairs—you see a garage? That girl's had troubles enough; she doesn't need you on top of it. People have been known to hire help, you know. So is that what you and your girlfriend talk about—what you're going to do if one of you dies? Last I knew, this was a public street, not a private stage. You don't have a hell of a lot to offer a woman, do you?

But that was all random, pointless: he'd said what he'd said, and he hadn't cooked in years, but he was sure he'd figure it out, and it wasn't about cooking anyway. He knew that as well as he knew that he couldn't even imagine touching her nightgown and bathrobe, or going into her purse for her house keys, or looking at whatever it was she kept in her bathroom drawer. He heard Kevin come up the stairs, and wondered for the first time if he ought to ask them if they wanted something of hers. Eventually he'd have to deal with her things, he supposed, or he'd have to let somebody else do it—Róisín or Norah or Fionnuala. One of them, one day, would phone him and say she'd be over to help him get sorted. When his mother died, a neighbor woman had taken care of that for him. He'd gone away, and had come back to an apartment that held only his own things.

Kevin watched himself unbuttoning his shirt in the mirror of the guest-room dresser. If his father decided to stay here, there'd be more of this. This what? He sighed, and wondered if the ghost of Rachel would ever get out of his head. This disorder, he answered her. Disorder, she said back. He unbuttoned his cuffs and looked himself in the eye. What am I supposed to do—wad it up to prove I love life? Buy three chairs for a man with no place to put them, just so he won't forget that he's the only one here? He took the shirt off and hung it on the back of the rocking chair, and the image of his mother, tidy at last before they closed the coffin, didn't come to him until he'd finished flossing in the bathroom, and he narrowed his eyes at himself in that mirror: Unfair, and you know it. The image of his father in one of Jimmy's lawn chairs, with Jimmy and Fionnuala in the other two, in the warm dusk, the bitter rage that picture brought, didn't come until he was in the bed.

In the backyard, Jimmy whistled "Galway Bay," beginning to end. They'd had a guy sing it at the funeral—it was a song of her girlhood, and she'd sung it to them when they were little. It was funny, he thought, pretending the melody didn't bring tears pricking in his eyes, how it got you: out there today he and Fionnuala had gone into a gift shop near the big fort at the end of the island, and he'd found himself looking at a knitted scarf, thinking he wished he could afford it for his mother. Kevin had that part right: ever since he finished high school, he'd been wishing he could afford things, but he hadn't managed it yet, had he? Yet. Well, Kevin seemed pretty sure he never would. He shook his head and gave up on the sky, where clouds were pale now against the dark. He stood and folded his chair, folded the other one, and stood wondering where to put them. The laundry room for now, he thought. Hell, if his father didn't want them, he'd give them to Fionnuala.

Lyle adjusted his pillow. After his mother died, he'd gone away to here, to Mary at her father's house in Oranmore. It had seemed sensible to him at the time, to buy an airplane ticket that cost a month's salary and fly to a country he'd never seen to visit a girl he'd met only three times and kissed once. He shifted in the bed, thinking what a ridiculous chance he'd taken. What if she hadn't been there? He hadn't even written to tell her he was coming. Well, she had been there, standing at the gate.

He turned over again and tried to stop it there: it had all worked out. But instead of Mary at the gate, he remembered the sly face of the old man outside the shop in Oranmore when he'd asked if there was a taxi, and how the old man had muttered and mumbled, shaking his head and pointing here and there, while Lyle stood there, helpless, finally desperate, and eventually paid the man ten American dollars for the stupid bicycle.

He sat up in the bed and yanked at the twisted blanket, and lay back down hard, his clumsiness on that bicycle vivid again in his muscles and bones, the rutted road clear in his mind, the wrong turn, the vicious dog rushing at him vivid, the heat—he'd worn a suit, he was that big an idiot, a suit and tie and dress shoes, all he was missing was a bouquet of flowers (and he'd almost had that, he remembered, half thought in the train station in Galway that maybe he should buy flowers, the first moment of doubt he'd had in the whole stupid trip)—what a laugh they must have had at him, the goddamned Yank with mud on his fancy clothes wobbling all over Ireland on a decrepit bicycle looking for the girl of his dreams—

He threw the blanket back and lunged out of the bed, stalked into the bathroom and slammed the door shut behind him. He'd made a complete spectacle of himself, hadn't he, and for what? To end up here, pissing in the dark, his sons talking about how pathetic he was, and he was, goddamn it, pathetic; he flushed the toilet and put the seat down by habit and then slammed it back up so hard it bounced back down.

Downstairs, holding in his hand the four stones Fionnuala's younger boy, Barry, had given him from the beach—and remembering the shy way he'd named the colors, as if colors were a wonder—Jimmy heard the door slam and listened to see what it meant. When he heard the second confused slamming, he dropped the stones and lurched toward the stairs, thinking his father had fallen, but then came the sound of his father's bathroom door opening, his father's feet crossing the small bedroom, and Jimmy stopped. He picked up the stones and arranged them on the end table, folded the couch out and undressed. Now that the stones were dry, they were dull, one reddish, one blue-gray, one vaguely green, and the last one, which had been so white, was as yellow as an old tooth. He lay down and turned off the light. It wasn't late yet, but he'd been out in the air all day, and he was tired, a good tired: he thought if he waked early enough and it was a nice day, he'd walk to the cemetery before they were up, take these stones. Enough ifs, there, Jim? he asked himself, and changed it: he'd wake early, and if it was raining, he'd call a cab. And if his father had fallen? He turned over, but it stayed: if Kevin was right?

So when the first of the fireworks went up just after midnight, from a boat well out in Galway Bay, all three of the Sullivans were still awake, but none of them saw that burst of green and silver against the brief dark of the summer sky. Their curtains were drawn, the doors locked, their thoughts far from the slow, spangling blossoms of red and blue, the brilliant white tracers, the reverent chorus of approval that rose from the group of American art students on the boat's deck. Even the distant thuds of the tiny finale, even the echoes of that noise, were long faded before Jimmy wandered into sleep, and then Kevin, too, crossed over, and finally, comforted on the edge of sleep by a thought of walking alone in the cemetery, Lyle slept.

THREE

The short night passed, the dawn's light came and grew, and the men slept on, well past their separate plans to be up early.

Although he'd been the last to sleep, Lyle was the first to wake. He moved quietly about the kitchen, letting Lady out, finding his notepad and tape measure, letting Lady in, and then he was out, alone, in the morning, unaware yet of how the walk up Prospect Hill would tire him, unaware, too, that as the door closed behind him, his older son woke in the room where Mary had fallen.

Long before he'd actually gone into sleep, Kevin had become ashamed, in a way that was so familiar as to be nearly a comfort. He had recalled his words to his brother, planning to be proud of them, and instead had known them to be spiteful, to have arisen from his own embarrassments. So by the time he woke, his wish to shame his brother and father by visiting the cemetery without them had softened into a wish to visit his mother's grave and apologize. He paused outside the closed door of his father's bedroom and heard no sound, and went shoeless down the stairs and past the open door to the living room, where Jimmy lay sleeping. He moved quietly about the kitchen, letting Lady out, finding the spare house key where it had been his whole life, always in a flowered saucer on the windowsill over the kitchen sink, in Littleton and then in Bentleyville and now in Galway, letting Lady in, checking the map for the simplest route to the cemetery, and then he was out, alone, in the morning. He was ravenously hungry, and decided to stop in town for a quick breakfast, maybe at the Supermac, if everything else was already crowded.

The morning sun was bright through the kitchen window by the time Jimmy woke—past ten—and he let Lady out and stood in the doorway eating a banana, deciding whether to walk or take a cab. He'd promised himself the walk if the weather was good, and though it would take longer, he decided to keep the promise, and not risk waking the others by making a phone call. He let Lady back in, and then, remembering that he'd been the last one in last night, and if he weren't there when they got up, they might worry, he moved quietly about the kitchen, found paper and pen, wrote a quick note (*Gone for a walk—nice morning! Jim*), and then he was out, alone, in the day, unaware yet that Barty would stop at the foot of Prospect Hill and give him a lift, unaware that he closed the door behind him on no one but Lady.

So all three of them made their ways through the city and

up the hill, each of them beginning in certainty and growing more doubtful as the cemetery came closer.

Lyle had passed a group of retired American schoolteachers in Kennedy Park (you could tell retired American schoolteachers, he believed, by their sensible shoes and the fact that one of them had a list of something that the others crowded around to look at), and as he trudged up the hill with the sun hot on his head and shoulders, he was certain they'd show up at the cemetery, hunting for Lady Gregory's grave.

Kevin had made a wrong turn after he'd parked the car, and accidentally discovered a small restaurant, Du Journal, its door open onto the street so he could see that there were empty tables. He'd had a cup of coffee and an excellent croissant, and the temptation had been strong to simply stay—read one of the newspapers, have another cup of coffee. As he was paying his bill, he overheard a family planning to find the graves of their forebears this morning; he was certain, driving up the hill, that they'd arrive soon after he did, hunting for the graves of Murphys, photographing one another next to headstones.

Only Jimmy, thanking Barty for the lift at the foot of the steep driveway into the cemetery, admitted what they all felt: "I don't know," he said, his hand still on the side of the truck, "the whole thing feels just that little bit stupid."

Barty shook his head, agreeing. "But we do it," he said.

"Yup," Jimmy said. "Thanks again," he said, and gave the truck a soft slap, and turned and walked up between the gateposts into the New Cemetery.

Lyle, who had had no breakfast and so little sleep, had arrived at the cemetery exhausted, and a little frightened by his exhaustion. He walked almost twice this distance every day by the bay; that the hill—which had never seemed so long when he'd come by taxi, to tend the grave of Mary's parents—could wind and weary him so made him feel frail, elderly. He managed the last bit, up into the cemetery itself and to the low brick step beside a small monument, on sheer embarrassment: he didn't want to be seen near collapse on the sidewalk, with cars going by. He lowered himself onto the step and wished, as he often had, that there were a bench or two somewhere in this cemetery. He had often rested on this step, just this uncomfortably, after weeding or planting at the Curtin grave, a duty he'd taken on the second year they'd been here. Róisín had wanted to cover the grave with colored gravel, like the white stone that was here, around the graves of the victims of a long-ago plane crash, but they'd talked her out of it. That first year he'd put in a nice bed of marigolds and alyssum, and then he'd added to it every season, so now there were jonquils and daffodils early, annuals in a different pattern every year for Cemetery Sunday in August, when Mary's brothers came back, and then the mums came on for fall.

He stretched his legs out in front of him. He'd caught his breath now, and realized that he was shaky at least partly from hunger and partly because two miles uphill with traffic alongside and no Lady to control his pace was a very different thing from two miles along the bay with a good breeze and a small dog. He'd be all right, he thought, and the fear—which had been, really, that Mary's death hadn't been freakish, inexplicable, but, in fact, timely—passed away, and he saw again that it was a bright midday in July, a good day for gardening. He'd met a number of people when he worked up here, mostly men, doing the same work for their families, and they'd talked a little now and then, admired something, shared extra plants, mentioned the weather. They'd never actually introduced themselves, only meeting once or twice a year, by chance; Lyle assumed they knew him as he knew them, by the names on the stones of the graves they tended—Ganon, Murphy, Anderson, Lally. For a moment he wished that today some one of them might be here, and not know what had happened, and so treat his presence as ordinary. If that happened—if, say, the quiet fellow who did such a nice job on the Hynes plot happened to be here, and happened to say, Fine days we're having—he could just agree, and go on to the Curtin grave and weed for a while, rest on his knees there in the quiet. He needn't go any farther than that.

He needn't go any farther than this, really. He was in

nobody's way right here; the small monument belonged to nobody. He knew its inscription inadvertently, from having rested here before: MAY ETERNAL PEACE BE THEIRS, and on the other side, IN MEMORY OF ALL THOSE WHO LOST THEIR LIVES ON BOARD THE DUTCH AIRLINER "HUGO DE GROOT" OVER THE ATLANTIC OCEAN ON AUGUST 14, 1958. On his first trip to Ireland, Mary had brought him to visit her mother's grave, and they'd stopped here for a few minutes. The monument had still been new then. Mary had told how one of the victims of the crash had been a little baby, and that rescuers had at first glance believed the baby was still alive, because it was smiling, there in the cold water of Galway Bay. She'd had tears in her eyes, telling that, and now, remembering, he wondered, as he never had before, whether the baby's marker was one of the "Unidentified" or one of the "Reinterred in Home Country."

He heard a car door slam at the foot of the driveway. He'd better get moving somewhere, he thought: that was probably the schoolteachers, and they'd be sure that this memorial was Lady Gregory's. He stood up and glanced down the driveway, and when he saw Jimmy, he was certain he'd been followed—discovered, trailed, the feeble, pathetic father to be saved from his own foolishness—and he knew that if he sat back down, Jimmy might well not see him, with the memorial between them. Or he could step around the memorial and tell him to go to hell.

But something about the way Jimmy was coming up the drive—kicking gently at stones as he walked, his head down and a little cocked, as if he were thinking, not hunting for his decrepit father—and something in the expression on his face made him look too much like a child to yell at. As Lyle watched, he remembered a picnic in a park, once, long ago, when both boys were very young. They'd been almost ready to go home when a brief thunderstorm drove them into one of the shelters. At first the rain had come off the roof in sheets, and the boys had shouted, giddy with the noise of the storm and the dash under the roof. When it stopped, as suddenly as it had begun, drops of water trickled and fell with whispers you could hardly hear, and the boys went quiet. Soon the sun came out and lit up the water beads like diamonds on every blade of the green grass. The next thing was the birds started to sing in the heart of a tree nearby, and the boys stepped out from under the roof as if they were stepping into a new-made world. Jimmy had that same hushed, bemused look on his face now, as he passed his father without seeing him, looking at something he held in the palm of his hand.

And Mary had taken Lyle's hand that day in the park, the two of them watching their sons, and she had said, Isn't it grand for me and you, Lyle. Isn't it surely grand for you and me.

At the top of the cemetery, Jimmy turned to the right and

Lyle could no longer see him. Up there was the Curtin grave, where the interlaced knot design of light and dark pansies would need weeding. Jimmy wouldn't notice, not the pattern or the weeds—he'd just keep going where he was going.

Lyle's intention this morning had been to measure and take notes about the sun and begin planning the garden he would make there in the fall. He'd had a plan for the red garden at the house—a ruby garden, for their fortieth anniversary, as a present to her. Last night he'd thought he could just adapt it for up here. Well, he couldn't be measuring and all that with Jimmy up there, could he. He patted his pockets. That was all ruined, for today.

The raw hump of dirt that was Mary's grave rose vivid in his mind. Even if Jimmy hadn't showed up, Lyle had gone as far as he was going to go today, he knew that now. He might as well start walking back home. He turned, and then he saw Kevin getting out of his car across the road. He watched him lock the car and put the keys in his pocket, look over at the cemetery and straighten his shoulders, and when Kevin lifted his chin and smoothed his throat with two quick passes of his hand, Lyle recognized in his son his own reluctance, and understood that each of them had come here alone, as if secretly, and he wanted to protect his sons, from one another, from himself, from the embarrassment of discovery.

Across the driveway and down a walk was the chapel. He'd never been inside it, didn't even know if it was kept locked, but if he headed for it, as if he meant to go inside, as if he meant to pray there, Kevin might see him from behind and turn back, believing he himself hadn't been seen.

Later, months later, Lyle would remember this moment and see that there had been something comic in his sense that it was a desperate plan, something ridiculous in his trembling urgency—but in this moment of fierce tenderness for these young men who had been boys when their mother took his hand in a rain-drenched park, he stepped around the monument and crossed the driveway in a kind of despairing hope, as if he were a civilian decoy sent to distract a sniper. He forced himself to keep his head bowed, to resist looking to the left, up to where Jimmy must be standing. If Jimmy happened to glance down the slope, he, too, might see Lyle, might see Kevin, too, and walk on, take the outside path, hidden among the tall crosses, and so make his way back to the entrance unseen.

Slowly, Lyle told himself: slowly. He must not reach the door of the chapel before Kevin had seen him.

Years later, sitting through Cemetery Sunday mass outside this same chapel, he would wonder if they had seen him, if the plan had worked. What he knew for certain was that the chapel door was unlocked when he reached it, and that inside it was cool and dim, and that when he came out, the only people he could see were a family of Americans wandering among the graves. He knew, too, that none of them ever mentioned having been there that day.

He had walked back down the hill almost as far as Eyre Square when Kevin pulled up beside him in the car and rolled down the window and offered him a lift, which he accepted, but Kevin didn't ask where he'd been, and he didn't ask where Kevin had been. And when they came upon Jimmy walking steadily down Queen Street and pulled up beside him, what Kevin said was, "Hey, Jim—we're going to get some lunch—come along?" And Jimmy grinned and said, "Sure," and climbed into the backseat, and never said where he'd been, or asked how they came to be out together.

The sun shone through a thin rain as Kevin parked the car, and Lyle suggested Tigh Neachtain's, because it was just around the corner and had a decent lunch for reasonable money. He even said, as he had before, "It's a real Irish pub—crowded, cramped, smoky—local color," and, in his relief that there'd be no conversation about the morning, he chuckled after he'd said it.

The several small rooms that made up Neachtain's were all full, packed, it seemed, with other people who had come in out of the suddenly heavy rain. Jimmy went to the left, into the room that ended with a fireplace, and Kevin to the right, through the front barroom and up the step into the narrow last room, looking without success for an empty table, and then the three of them stood in the doorway near the snugs and the smaller bar, deciding.

"It wouldn't be this bad except for the rain," Lyle said. He was so hungry now that the idea of walking around trying to find a less crowded place for lunch made him light-headed.

"And the tourists," Kevin said, and he was right: many of the little tables held cameras or shopping bags instead of food or drink.

"They always get a lunch crowd," Lyle said. "Year-round."

Kevin turned his palm up in apology. "When the rain lets up, we could go back down to that fish place," he offered.

Jimmy nodded. "Fish and chips," he said.

And they might have done that, despite the rich, sausagey smell of the lunch here, except that a wiry old man who stood near them with a glass of Guinness in one hand and a cigarette between the fingers of the other turned just then and squinted at Lyle. "I seen you about," he said. "You take the pretty little dog down the prom mornings."

Lyle nodded.

The man sipped his Guinness and stepped closer, so they were a foursome blocking the doorway. He gestured with his head toward the snug beside them. "Ye might not have so much of a wait," he said confidentially. "They're after having a row." He winked.

Jimmy, the only one of them who had given the man more than a glance, grinned. "What about?" he said.

The man touched Lyle's shoulder with the back of the hand that held his stout. "Your sons?" he said, and when Lyle again nodded, he transferred his glass to his cigarette hand, and said, "Patrick O'Connell," and extended his free hand to Jimmy. And because Jimmy took the hand, and said "Jim Sullivan," Kevin and Lyle had no choice but to follow suit.

The introductions completed, Patrick O'Connell leaned even closer, his smoke in their faces, and said, "Your man lost a fair bit on the dogs last night," and nodded toward the snug again, just as another old man, also on the thin side, came out of the snug with his head down and pushed past them and out the door to the street. He was followed immediately by a woman of like age, but taller.

"You," she said to Patrick as he stepped back, both hands raised a little, to let her pass, "you're just as bad," and she, too, went out the street door.

Kevin twisted to peer after her and then turned back to the others, his face tense. "Rain's let up," he said.

Jimmy flipped his hand at the snug. "Table's free," he said.

"Me brother Tommy," Patrick O'Connell said, as if the quarreling couple still stood there, "and his lovely wife."

"Jesus Christ," Lyle muttered. He stepped into the snug and sat on the far side of the table, on the bench built to the wall. Kevin followed, and slid onto the other bench, and Jimmy leaned in the doorway and said, "Everybody wants the sausage thing?"

"Whatever," Kevin said, smoothing the sides of his hair with his palms, and Lyle said, "Fine—you got money?" but Jimmy was gone.

Later, sitting under the stars in the lawn chairs, Jimmy would decide not to tell them how Patrick O'Connell stayed with him, and when he'd ordered the three plates of sausage casserole and stood waiting, Patrick said, "You're from America," and Jimmy said, "Yeah—I live in Ohio, in the Midwest."

Patrick nodded; the cigarette had disappeared, and now he drained his glass and stared into it. "And it's your holiday," he said.

Jimmy looked at him. "No," he said. "A visit."

Patrick nodded again without looking up. "And your mother, then."

Jimmy waited, and Patrick met his eyes. "She died," Jimmy said. "On Saturday."

Patrick put his hand on Jimmy's shoulder. "Mary Curtin that was," he said. "I knew her when she was a girl. I'd see her these past years in the shops—a happy woman," he said, "and young."

Now, in the snug, after a long silence in which Lyle felt he could almost hear Kevin's mind working, the tense disapproval on his face was so active, Kevin said, "Snug. I suppose in the winter it is, but, boy—these benches don't really give you much room."

Before Lyle could reply, Patrick O'Connell was back: he took the two dirty pint glasses from the table without looking at Lyle and Kevin and was gone again.

"Does that guy work here, or is he some friend of yours?" Kevin said.

"I've seen him," Lyle said.

Kevin adjusted himself on the narrow bench.

"You're expected to sit forward," Lyle said. "Elbows on the table beside your pint."

"Seems pretty early in the day," Kevin said, meaning the idea of a pint and probably Patrick O'Connell's pint in particular, but Jimmy reappeared just then with three glasses of beer, so it stood for that, too. "I mean, it's only twelve-thirty," he said to Jimmy. "Don't they have water?"

"It's beer," Jimmy said. "Got to have beer with sausage."

And in fact the beer looked good, golden in the glasses, and Lyle felt his thirst as if the color of the beer had called it up. "Thanks," he said.

Jimmy pulled silverware wrapped in paper napkins from his hip pocket. "No problem," he said, and turned, and there behind him, a new cigarette tilted from his mouth, was Patrick O'Connell, a plate of lunch in either hand and a third balanced on his forearm.

"You'll join us," Lyle said—again, he seemed to have no choice—as Jimmy took the plates and set them on the table.

But Patrick shook his head. "Ah, no," he said, "I never eat on the empty stomach."

Jimmy shook Patrick's hand, and for a second it looked like the old man meant to embrace him, but he only gave his arm a pat, spilling ash onto the floor, nodded to the others, and turned away, and Jimmy sat on the small stool.

The rain had stopped and people might have left, but if so, more had come in, and people passed the door of the snug with plates and pints, and the noise hadn't diminished at all. Still, for a moment inside the snug, a kind of silence fell.

Lyle lifted his glass. "Sláinte," he said. "Irish for

'cheers.'" The beer was fine and sharp in his throat, and he drank down almost half in that first draft.

They ate. Once their first hunger was past, they talked about what time they were expected at Róisín's that night for the good-bye supper, and how early they'd have to set off in the morning to make their planes—Kevin's was earlier by almost two hours—and whether Jimmy needed to do laundry before they went. They'd just agreed to stop in Sheridan's shop and get some cheese to take to Róisín, and Kevin had stacked their empty plates, when the second round arrived, three whiskeys carried by Patrick O'Connell. He bent to set the glasses on the table, and before they could protest, he straightened and looked Lyle right in the eye, his own face solemn. "I'm sorry for your trouble," he said.

"Thank you," Lyle said. It was what one said, after all.

Patrick bowed his head and raised it again, a quick prayer or a slow nod. "You've a fine pair of sons," he said. "You're a lucky man after all." He nodded his head again, and was gone.

"You told him?" Kevin demanded, his face pale.

Jimmy shook his head and lifted the stacked plates. "He already knew. He said he knew her, and he figured out who we were." He stood, took the three empty beer glasses and the plates, and left the snug.

Kevin snorted. "He knew her," he said. "Old drunk."

Patrick O'Connell's directness had touched Lyle, and the

"fine pair of sons" had brought back the two of them as skinny little boys in that rainy park: he pinched the bridge of his nose to stop the prickle of tears. "She grew up here, Kevin," he said. "A lot of people knew her." He wished Kevin were a more tolerant man, and he glanced at him, and saw his own motion, thumb and forefinger, repeated.

"Jesus," Kevin said.

Jimmy came back and stood in the doorway. "So are we going or staying?"

Lyle lifted his whiskey. "Sláinte," he said, and drank.

Jimmy shoved his hands into his pockets, and then took them out again and went back to the bar and returned with three pints of lager, and sat down. He moved his whiskey half an inch, and moved it back. They'd quarrel now, Lyle thought, the same old quarrel, of Kevin's caution and Jimmy's lack of it.

"Tommy and Paddy O'Connell were bold boys," Kevin said.

None of them moved. Kevin sat looking at the top of the snug wall, Jimmy at the wetness on the table, Lyle at Kevin's face: all of them were listening, waiting.

"No way," Jimmy said, finally.

"As like as two peas in a pod," Kevin said. He lowered his gaze to his whiskey. "But the one, Paddy it was, had a terrible fear of the dark."

Jimmy put his hand to his forehead, shielding his eyes.

"And his brother had a fear of thunder." He said, "I do not believe it."

Kevin leaned forward and put one palm flat against each side of the short glass, and the silence among them returned until he said, quickly now, almost fiercely, "There came a night when they'd left their football out in the yard, and when bedtime came they couldn't find it, and Paddy said, You must go out and fetch it, Tommy, and Tommy was just at the door when the thunder began far off." He turned the glass between his palms. "I can't do this."

Jimmy brought his whiskey glass to his mouth and then put it back down, and then lifted it again and drank before he said, "And neither of them dared go out, even though they called each other coward and baby, and then a terrible rain came." He cleared his throat. "And the ball was ruined, and they were poor enough, and so they had no ball after that."

They had the words wrong, of course, but Lyle remembered her telling it, how she'd shake her head as if the football in the back garden were a terrible shame. The rain lashing down, she'd probably said, and, Right enough, that was the end of the two of them being show-offs on the football pitch. He drank from his pint, and was glad he'd been decent to Patrick O'Connell, who didn't, in fact, seem like a man afraid of the dark at all. Maybe careless of his possessions. And then he drank again, because the wish to say that to her was so strong—I met Paddy O'Connell today, he'd say, and she'd say, Did you, now? and he'd let a minute or two pass, and then he'd say, That story you used to tell the boys about the football—is that the same Paddy O'Connell?

"It's like meeting Tom Sawyer or something," Kevin said, and he and Jimmy laughed, tentatively.

"There was another one, too—remember? About the birthday party?"

"When Tommy was so afraid of the thunder he had to go and lie on the stairs—did you ever understand that?"

"I think it was that the stairs were in the middle of the house, so he was as far inside as he could get."

"I always thought it was just that he wasn't such a big shot. That always seemed the point of the stories about Paddy and Tommy O'Connell—there was the one about them going to the races."

"Ah, it was the Galway Race Week, and weren't those bold lads—that's it, she always called them 'bold lads'— weren't those bold lads ready to burst with the excitement of it? And—wait, wait—" Jimmy laughed and shook his head. "I don't remember anything except the beginning."

"They refused to change into their good clothes, and so the money fell out of their pockets," Lyle said.

"Yeah," Jimmy said. "Yeah."

"Well," Lyle said. He lifted his whiskey. "To Paddy and Tommy O'Connell."

"To the bold lads," Jimmy agreed, and they drank.

Kevin leaned back. "I wonder why he wasn't at the funeral."

"I think he was at the wake, actually," Jimmy said. "He looked familiar, you know?"

"There were a lot of people there," Lyle said. "I wouldn't be surprised."

"I wonder if Niamh Duffy was there," Jimmy said.

"Niamh Duffy with the long red hair," Kevin said. "I used to have a picture of her in my head that was half fairy tale and half Playboy Bunny."

"Niamh Duffy was the patron saint of my boyhood," Jimmy said. "Ye never know, do ye, how a thing will come round—that was the moral of Niamh Duffy every time."

Lyle nodded. "Never too late," he said.

"She became a nun," Kevin said. "That was the moral—"

"No, no—she was the homeliest girl and she grew up to be a beauty—"

"Sure, okay, sure—and she fought with all the boys like a lad herself, and then wasn't she the one that started kissing them—" Kevin smiled and drank from his pint. "That's what I always saw—Niamh Duffy snogging on the footpaths."

"Sister Niamh Duffy to you, bud," Jimmy said.

Maybe, while they were laughing, Jimmy signaled the barman for three more whiskeys, though Lyle didn't see it happen. They laughed, and the freedom of their laughter then should have led one of them to say, I guess I've had enough, but none of them did. Jimmy went to the bar and brought them back three more small ones.

"But I'm sure there weren't any nuns at the funeral home," Kevin said.

"The Poor Clares are cloistered," Lyle said. "She couldn't have been there."

"Ye never know, do ye?" Jimmy said.

Lyle said, "So did you ever think about being a priest?" which set them off again. "I mean, because of Niamh Duffy," he explained.

"Oh, I was heartbroken," Kevin said, still chuckling, "but not that bad."

Jimmy, too, shook his head. "It's funny—I don't think I ever made the connection. I mean, we had priests, right? But the nuns we had didn't seem to be the same kind of nuns."

"Right—hers were all like saints or something—maybe it was the names, those Latin names—Sister Pacifica, Sister Benedict?"

"Or the habits. The only place I ever saw nuns in habits was over here."

"Oh, remember when we went to Bunratty that time?" Kevin said.

"And we met those two nuns in the castle, and I thought they were witches?"

"Sorceresses, I thought," Kevin said. "I was scared to death."

"Ah, those little nuns'll never harm ye. She always called nuns 'little,' you know?"

"Not *our* nuns—not Sister Mary Ambrose."

As Neachtain's grew nearly quiet outside the snug, they told each other the stories they had from her. They told about Niamh Duffy mocking the sisters, and her contraband lipstick, and how she rescued her little brothers from the bullies, and how she went to Hollywood and came back a nun, after all those mad things she'd done, and wasn't she in the Poor Clares to this very day? When Kevin came back from the bar with fresh pints, they told about the man who'd raised a rook from the egg and claimed it could talk, and about Big Bob who'd seen a sheep killed and became Oranmore's first vegetarian, and about the deaf woman who played the whistle like an angel, and they told three stories they couldn't quite remember involving priests and drink. They told her story about the miraculous Christmas Eve fire and another about a fire that killed a whole family, and in every story they tried to use her words, though they seldom mentioned her, and told no stories about her that day. That day in Neachtain's, it was enough for them to half sense her voice, her talk, hovering nearby as they grew slowly and slightly drunk together in the afternoon.

The drunkenness took them all by surprise. Jimmy

stood up from his stool and reached for the side of the snug doorway.

"You okay?" Kevin said.

Jimmy turned and grinned back at them over his shoulder. "Not quite," he said. "But I'm not driving—you are."

"I believe," Kevin said, "that driving would be unwise. And I believe I have had enough. Dad?"

Lyle nodded. "I think we'd better do some serious walking before we have to face Aunt Róisín," he said, and all of them laughed and were still laughing when they stepped out into the surprising daylight of the street, where the rain had stopped again, and a rook hurried along the pavement, and in that moment of reorienting themselves to the lay of this land, the way the three men stepped and turned, still smiling, might have been taken as a kind of dance, the three of them taken as men dancing.

They sobered up over Róisín's dinner, slept well enough, and Kevin and Jimmy left on time in the morning. Their father's parting words were, "Keep your noses clean," and they repeated that in the car on the drive to Shannon, grinning, shaking their heads; it was so typical, what they should have expected, after all. When they'd returned the car and checked in, promised to stay in touch, gripped each other's hands, and Kevin was walking away down the concourse, Jimmy called it softly after him—"Keep your nose clean!"—and Kevin raised his hand in acknowledgment without turning around. It was a good parting, all things considered.

At the pay phone, as Jimmy dialed Fionnuala's number, the patient, wailing cry of a child far down the concourse reached and lifted him back into the air, flying—that was his memory, that his mother flew, hurtled through the air, he suspended behind her by her hold on his hand—down a mall to the little boy crouched wailing at the top of the escalator. The memory was so urgent, so involuntary, that when Fionnuala answered, he didn't say, Hey—I just wanted to say good-bye. Instead he said, "Listen—one time—I must have been five or so—my mother and I were at the mall," and the details of the memory returned in the telling. He told Fionnuala how his mother had knelt beside the little boy and spoken to him, and how he'd felt his own hand, released from hers, grow cool as he watched her fingers slide inside the boy's sneaker and slip his foot out of it. He remembered how he'd stood beside her with the cloth of her coat under his hand and despised the other boy for not wiping his nose, for having a dirty sock twisted on his foot. He blushed, telling her about his own mean satisfaction when the boy's mother rose up the escalator already yelling at him, and how his own mouth had gone dry when that other mother grabbed the still-crying boy by the shoulder and shook him, scolding—he'd run ahead of her to the escalator, he hadn't minded, wasn't he ashamed of himself, how many times did she have to tell him. Ah now, the ladeen's frightened enough, Jimmy's mother said, and the other woman—Jimmy remembered her as thin and blond and dressed like a teacher, maybe in a suit?—said, I'll be the judge of that, thank you just the same, and turned back to the boy and said, Now get your shoe on, what's the matter with you?

The story Jimmy told Fionnuala on the phone wasn't the one Mary had told later that day to Lyle, explaining in detail about the untied shoe, the drooping shoelace, the care that escalators required of boys. He told instead the story as he felt it there in the airport, with her a week dead: the magnificence of his mother's sympathy and patience and courage, how she'd knelt there in the busy mall and worked that shoelace out of the teeth of the escalator steps, how she'd put her arms around that little boy right in front of his mother, and told him that he'd be fine now, he'd be fine, and then, waiting for the bus, when Jimmy leaned on her lap and said, Why was that lady so mad? how she'd said, There's mothers and there's mothers, and wiped her eyes.

Remembering and then, almost violently, knowing her scent and the texture of her skin and the contours of her body, he had nearly forgotten that he was telling, that anyone was listening, until Fionnuala said, "Oh, Jimmy," and he knew she was crying, and he cleared his throat and said, "Listen—I'm coming back—you know that, right? Before Christmas, I'll be back."

And at that moment, in the sky over the Atlantic, as the flight attendant passed a cup of tea to the woman beside Kevin and the woman reached to accept it, the mingled scents of tea and perfume lifted Kevin and set him down in the kitchen in Littleton, glaring at the blue teapot on the table to keep from looking at his mother, who was too beautiful that morning. The woman went on with the story she'd been telling, how she'd been to Ireland for the first time a few years ago, when her late husband was very ill, and she'd loved Aran so much that she'd come back, now that her children were grown, to try to buy a small house on one of the islands, and had failed. She was a handsome woman, and calmly cheerful, despite the disappointment, and Kevin kept up his part of their conversation, but beneath it, that morning so long ago went on, too. He'd complained of the toast being cold and his favorite shirt not clean—he must have been eight or nine—and his mother had laughed and said, Ah, you'd want jam in your egg, Kevin. Gross, he'd said, but he'd refused to laugh: it wasn't right that she had on earrings and lipstick at breakfast, when Daddy was out of town and he and Jimmy had school.

While the woman justified the islanders' unwillingness to sell, Kevin struggled again to find a reason for his mother's being dressed up—a doctor's appointment, a funeral, something at the church. He knew, as his grown self, that it must have been something like that, but he could feel still his sullen boy self wanting to insult her, and at the same time wanting to walk with her into whatever roomful of people waited to see her so bright and pretty.

The memory was vivid, but when the woman said, I think, though, that things turn out for the best—I don't believe I'll need to come back again, and asked about him, had he been in Ireland on business, he didn't tell her that story. He couldn't say how he'd betrayed his mother that day, pretending stomach cramps, manufacturing a cold sweat, or how he'd sobbed when she brought him ginger ale after he'd gone back to bed and she'd seen Jimmy off on the school bus, whatever innocent plan she'd had for that day ruined.

And he couldn't tell the woman that his mother had died a week ago, or that just now, here at thirty thousand feet, she'd been so real, for a moment, that he'd known the smell of herself behind the perfume and the exact flesh of her hand on his forehead. He said instead that he'd been visiting his parents, that he came two or three times a year. The woman nodded and asked if he came at Christmas usually, and she smiled and admitted that she had a romantic notion of Christmas in Ireland. And maybe because he'd been remembering himself as a dissembling child, who had succeeded—his mother had kept her earrings and blue dress on all day as he watched television and developed the stomachache he'd pretended, and she had been kind and merry with him—and grieved his success, he told this woman a story that hadn't happened.

"I was over last Christmas," he said, "with my fiancée. She's Jewish—my parents are Catholic, of course—and we were both pretty nervous. But my folks—my mother especially—they were fantastic. Amazing." With the telling of how it might have been, he remembered it all: how he and Rachel arrived in the evening, by surprise, took a taxi from the train station, and just showed up at the back door, and his mother's delight, the moment there at the door with the light rain in the air, the smells of his mother, his father, his beloved, himself—tea and earth and flowers and wool—and he was so certain of it, for the minutes of the telling, that when the woman said, "So your wife will come with you next winter," he said, "Yes—we'll be coming back."

And so, heading back to America, Mary's sons began repeating their father's wobbly ride, hoping, as he had, to find love leaning on a gate, a story they had never heard, a story he would never tell. He was finished with the past, its promises and failures: that much he had decided, that morning, on the edge of a quarrel with both his sons. They were right that he had a decision to make, a lot of decisions, actually, but all of them had to do with the future, his future— their futures, he had decided, watching them drive off, were their business, and his future was his. And right now he was doing the math.

Once the boys had driven away, he had found his tape and measured the distance from the back door to the back of the yard. Then he had walked that distance six times, counting his steps, and then he had divided to discover the average length of his stride, and then he had written that number— 34 inches—in his small notebook, and then he had leashed Lady and begun walking. He had counted his steps from his back door to the spot where he considered himself to have stepped onto the prom—755—and had stopped there and written that down. Then he had started again from one, and counted each step to the small rocky beach where he unleashed Lady and she began charging the waves, and he had written that number—3,017—in the notebook. When Lady came back and he snapped the leash back on, he began counting again, and when he reached the bench nearest his starting point, he took the notebook out again and sat down and wrote the new number—3,041—pleased already at how close the two numbers were. And right now, as a tall fellow in a tweed cap—clearly a tourist, since who'd wear tweed in July?—came and sat down at the other end of the bench, he was doing the math. He wanted to know whether he'd been right the other day, when he'd said five miles; he didn't like to think he'd been wrong, and then the walk up to the cemetery had tired him much more than he'd expected. He usually walked for about two hours; Lady being a small dog and therefore slowing his pace below the average of four miles an hour, he had been willing to estimate that he made about two and a half miles an hour, though he really thought he went faster than that, farther than that.

He just wanted to know. A mile was 5,280 feet, if his memory served him, times 12, for 63,360 inches, and his average stride was 34 inches, 34 into 63,360, so when the fellow in the tweed cap said, "Pretty dog you got there," Lyle only nodded, noticing that the man was American and roughly of his own generation, but continuing with his division: a mile was 1,863 of his strides.

"Well, it certainly turned out to be a nicer day than I'd expected," the man said. "Nice sunny day." He crossed his legs, and then crossed his arms, too. He sounded like he might be from Chicago, or Rochester—that kind of twang to his voice.

"It is," Lyle said. Add 3,017 and 3,041, for 6,058—divided by 1,863 wasn't going to give him anything like five.

"I tell you, everybody back home said bring a raincoat, bring an umbrella—rains all the time in Ireland. Won't get any tan over there, they said." The American chuckled, unfolded himself, gestured outward.

More like three.

"Course, that's not what I came over for, like I told them. I came over to see where I came from, if you know what I mean."

Three and just over a quarter—3.25, roughly. "I do," Lyle said. He circled the number, closed the notebook, and put the pencil and notebook in his shirt pocket.

The man chuckled again, took off his cap and looked into it. "You must get pretty sick of us Americans coming over for that—hunting up the ancestors, the old sod, all that."

Lyle looked at him then, at the shy apology in his face, and then leaned down and touched Lady's head, and then looked out across the bay. "Not at all, at all," he said. He stood, and Lady got up. He'd walk to the Claddagh, see what that came out to; lots of days, when it was this nice, he did that first, and that might well be another mile, mile and a half. He put out his hand to the American. "You're welcome so," he said, and smiled as they shook, and then he said to Lady, "Come along," and he was away.

The lock and latch work smoothly, but the front door has been so seldom used that it sticks at the top corner, and so Lyle bangs the wood once, sharply, with the side of his fist, to force it open. He has come to the front door, instead of the back, to begin as he intends to go on, with a kind of caution he could not explain, a kind of formality that seems to him fitting: to enter the house where he now lives alone, a widower, through the kitchen would have about it something slovenly, something leading to casual neglect, to eating from containers, to failing to shave, to piling newspapers in the corners. He has come to the front door, refusing to notice Lady's polite confusion, and now the door swings open into the small entryway, into the echo of the sound of his hand striking the door. Although the fine rain that began filling the air an hour ago continues to fall, and although he has been hurrying because of the rain and because he has walked longer than usual and the usual hour for his lunch is long past, he pauses before he steps into the house.

His sons disagree: Kevin has urged him to return to America, insisted on the practicality of that, and although

Lyle knows that Kevin is capable of self-interest, he knows, too, that Kevin feels a responsibility as the oldest son, as the stable son, and Lyle respects that. Jimmy has insisted that their father's decision is none of their business, and although Lyle knows that Jimmy, too, is capable of self-interest and chary of responsibility, he knows as well that Jimmy means to be respectful, in this, of his father's rights as an able adult, and Lyle is touched by that. He has walked, today, twice as long as usual, and he has reached no decision, has reached only the distant certainty that he cannot, yet, frame his own choices; twice today he has thought of Fionnuala saying, It's very soon.

So his pause here, in the soft, rainy air on his front doorstep, is not a moment of decision, but it is his first return. The house is empty, and so he pauses, and then Lady, tilting her head to glance at his face, puts one paw lightly over the threshold and stops.

Lyle grins. All right, he says, and they go in, and he closes the door behind them, and he says, I'm hungry, too, before the sound of the door closing can become an echo, before the silence can begin. Shake, he tells her, and she gives a quick shake there in the entry, where the floor is tiled. Good enough, he says, though he thinks he should maybe start keeping a small towel there, in the drawer of the table, so he can wipe off her feet when they come in. Come along, and they go down the hall, past the sitting room and the stairs, to the kitchen.

He unhooks the leash and hangs it on its hook, and he has opened the cupboard to get her treat when he remembers that he hasn't gotten a newspaper. He stands with his hand on the cupboard door and decides: without exactly remembering how frail he felt yesterday when he'd skipped breakfast, he decides he will make and eat a sandwich before he goes back out.

Outside this house in the afternoon it is July, and wind is gathering beneath the rain that falls, now, harder, pelting against windows and walls. This wind will last only a minute; it is the edge of the end of the rain, and the wind will clear the sky, leaving clouds that are high and light. In the bay, the sea endures the quick rain, and the wind is too weak to trouble even the tips of the waves.

Lyle bends to look into the refrigerator, remembering, vaguely, leftover chicken salad. He finds the yellow bowl, and takes it out and lets the refrigerator door shut as he lifts the foil from the top of the bowl and turns. Smell this, he says, and then he stands for a long time alone in his kitchen before he covers the bowl again and sets it carefully on the counter. In a moment, he will go into the laundry room and find an old towel and take it out to the entryway, and then he will come back to the kitchen and make himself tea and

toast, and then he will go back out, to the shop, for his newspaper, and when he comes back, it will no longer be his first
return. For now, though, for a long few minutes now, he
rests his hands on the counter beside the yellow bowl and
watches the rain blurring the back garden, and he waits for
the echo of his voice in the kitchen to fade.

8

THE HARD STAND

You forgot it was Thursday, and you've left the front door ajar, so you hear Róisín say, "Lyle?" barely a second before she appears in the sitting room and cries out, "Jesus Mary and Joseph, what are you about?"

And there you are: a seventy-year-old boy, caught in what a moment ago seemed perfectly innocent but is now revealed to you as a complete mess, and it's all you can do to keep from stammering back, N-nuthin', as you try to think just what it is you *are* about, and how it has come to this.

There's a heap of your dead wife's clothes on the couch, and there's a woman you don't quite know holding one of Mary's sweaters up to her own front, and there's you. And Róisín, Mary's sister, who seems to have deduced, both quickly and correctly, that you're not being robbed, although she recognizes that the woman is a Traveller, and you know what she thinks of Travellers. The alarm that made her pale when she first stepped into the room has given way already, in something like three seconds, to outrage, pure, simple, livid. "You," she says to the woman, and in her face an odd fear battles with the fury and half wins, so what comes out is, "There's been a misunderstanding here—you might go along now," and she makes a shooing motion with her hand. "Go along," she says again, because the woman hesitates. Whatever there was of fear dissipates before your very eyes, leaving the fury in complete command. "And leave that jumper where you found it!"

There's something of the cornered child in the Traveller woman's face, and a blush rising, and you know exactly (because it's what you're feeling) how a cornered child feels, so you manage to croak, "You can keep the sweater if you want it." You did invite *her* in, and you did tell her to see if there was anything in this lot she wanted; there will certainly be hell to pay with Róisín once the woman leaves, but it does seem to be the least you can do.

You know full well that's all you've been doing for the last two months, since your sons went back to the States after the funeral: the least you can do. Now, however, doesn't seem to be the moment to reflect on how badly you've managed your short career as a widower.

Your gallantry is a bit weak, a bit late, and apparently a bit misplaced. The woman lowers the sweater and then looks at it and then drops it, slowly, to the floor in front of her. She's a chunky, dark-haired, round-faced woman, prob-ably in her thirties, wearing a damp jacket—this is Ireland, everybody has a damp jacket—with nothing remarkable about her in the normal course of things, which is that she comes to your door about once a week and asks if you've got "anything extra." She never acts like she's begging; it's more like she's come to pick up your contribution. You've been giving her odd grocery items for two months—the bag with today's cans of soup and tuna sits right there beside the couch—and you hadn't really considered that offering her Mary's clothes might be a critical escalation of "extra." And now the sweater—it's gray, nothing particular about it that you know of, just a sweater you don't even remember Mary ever wearing—lies on the sitting-room floor between the Traveller woman and Róisín, and all three of you are look-ing at it.

"I wouldn't give it to a freezin' whore," the woman says, almost sweetly. She looks Róisín full in the face. "It's feckin' ugly as you are." She steps deliberately onto the sweater and scuffs it with her feet, making you think of the way your dog—the old dog, back in Ohio, Prince—the way he used to scratch up the leaves after he'd done his business, and you read somewhere that the purpose of that behavior was to spread his scent in order to deter predators and competitors. Scuff, scuff, scuff, and then she walks right at Róisín.

Róisín has gasped so loudly, so deeply, it's a wonder she

hasn't hyperventilated and fainted dead away, but she's no match for a scorned Traveller woman half her age, and she steps aside—far aside—and watches with you as the young woman departs, at a measured and dignified pace.

A long moment then ensues, within which there is no sound of the front door closing.

"Mother of God," Róisín says, but she's not looking at you yet. "What was in your mind?"

"I better close the door," you say.

"She'll mark it some way—mind you, that's how they are, these ones, now she's been offended," Róisín says. Her voice is flat grim. "You'll be robbed inside a week."

These ones" was the way she explained it to you a month ago, when she caught sight of this same woman walking away with the three cans of pork and beans you'd given her. You were on your knees in the backyard, just about to start planting that flat of white impatiens, and here came Róisín—uninvited then, too—through the gate, and she said, "Lyle, you're never after letting that tinker woman in the door, are you?" before she'd even got the gate open. Before you remembered that it was none of her business what you did or who you let in, you said, "Just in the front hall"—that is, you admitted it, and she was on it in a flash.

"And left her standing there looking about for whatever

she could slip into her pocket, or come back for later? No," she said, and waved her hand in the air. "Don't even think about it! It's right to give her something—Mary did it for years, though I told her it was daft, but if you stopped now, who knows how she'd take it? So that's all right, to give her bits and pieces, and they never seem to mind what it is, but here——" She turned and went in the back door that you'd left standing open so Lady—the dog you have now, who never does that spread-the-scent business old dead Prince did—could go in and out.

You'd gotten to your feet but you still stood there for a second, looking stupid, before you brushed the bits of grass off your knees and followed her in.

Not that you had much choice.

After Mary's death early in the summer, you got added to Róisín's schedule. You're expected on Sundays for noon dinner, and Thursdays she stops by before she drives out to the supermarket on the edge of town. You can't drive in this crazy country, wrong side of the road, steering wheel on the wrong side of the car, no shoulders anywhere—no sane person can. So that first Thursday, she said maybe you'd want to go with her, like Mary used to. You told her no, straight out, though you didn't tell her how some days the only human voice you heard was in the shops, Mrs. Duggan or John Ward talking to the odd customer, and you'd be damned if you'd trade that for the piped-in music in the aisles of Tesco.

The next week she stopped anyway, and said she thought you might need something—potatoes, say, or coal—that you'd have trouble carrying home. What she thought you'd do with fifty pounds of potatoes, alone in the house, or coal in July, or whatever giant thing she had in mind, you couldn't fathom. On the other hand, you figured she meant it kindly, so you thanked her, and said you'd let her know if the need came up, and she'd said she'd just call in on Thursdays in case.

But the day of the Traveller woman, you saw what the game was, really: she was checking up on you, on you in the house.

There she stood, in the kitchen she hadn't been invited into, her eyes darting around—has he taken to leaving the dishes in the sink, are the newspapers piling up, empty whiskey bottles lying about, is there a stink of garbage to the place—that is, is the fellow falling apart? Can he survive without his wife? Can any man survive without a woman?

But since she didn't actually ask those questions, you couldn't answer them. Instead you said, "What?"

She led you into your own laundry room. "There," she said, and lifted a plastic grocery bag from a hook behind the door. "This is what Mary did, you see? She'd the bag all ready, and when she saw that woman at the door she just came and got it, and handed it out to her."

She opened the bag, and you both looked in—a can of

peas, a box of vanilla cookies, a carton of cranberry juice—
and maybe she had the same swift vision of Mary herself
you had—Mary standing in the kitchen on a late-spring day
deciding what to put in, that way she'd scowl—because she
shut the bag up fast and hung it back where it had been, and
you both turned and went into the kitchen, as if you were
glad that was over.

She adjusted her glasses and sighed, as if she were being
extremely patient. "That's what you must do, to keep her
out of the house. Put together whatever seems sensible to
you, and hang it where you can just take it up and hand it
out." She mimed taking it up and handing it out, like you
were a two-year-old, or not a native speaker, and might not
understand the words otherwise. "Will you do that so?"

"I doubt she's a real menace," you said.

"You don't know with these ones—"

"You claim she's been coming to the door for years, and
we haven't had a robbery that I'm aware of."

"Ah, but you see, Mary never let her in the door, or never
did after the first time." She gave a bitter, satisfied little smile
and turned away, and you knew hanging the bag in the laundry room had been her idea in the first place.

"That *you* know of," you said, but you said it to her back,
because she'd walked right out of the kitchen and down the
little hall to the sitting room.

"I'm on my way to Tesco," she said, like that was news,

and as if she weren't noticing that the drapes were still closed and your dirty soup bowl and spoon from yesterday's lunch still sitting on the table beside your chair, "and I just wondered did you want anything." At least you'd taken the blanket back upstairs so that wasn't wadded on the couch for her to see.

"I'm fine," you said.

"Right so," she said, breezy as can be, "then I'm off—mind what I tell you about that woman. I'll just let myself out the front door."

Which she did, and left you standing there, again, like an idiot. You heard her car start up and pull away, and then, Johnny-on-the-spot, you said, "What the hell do you care if the place is a damned pigsty? You don't live here."

There you stood, waiting for Mary to come from the kitchen and say, Ah now, she's not so bad, like she always did when you mouthed off that way.

In fact, you have no memory of Mary letting the Traveller woman in or not letting her in, or mentioning that she existed. Apparently any number of things besides regular vacuuming and laundry went on right in front of you for years without you noticing it; you keep being surprised at how much you didn't pay any attention to. It's the same now: you watched your wife die, so you know it's true, but

you keep being ambushed by the feeling she's about to come
to the doorway and ask did you want tea. Almost every day
you turn to ask her something ordinary—are we out of
bread, where's my green shirt—and then for a long, hard
moment you have to go through it again, as if you can't
quite learn that she isn't here anymore. You never imagined
that the simple forward motion of days could be so
absolutely altered.

For all the years of your marriage, you see now, it was
Mary who made the days go that way, forward, simply. She'd
been a pale, eager, shy girl when you married her, pretty in
her way, nervous in company, and, she had claimed, not a
hard worker. You'd been the one with the job and the ambi-
tion, as far as it went. And that had been far enough for her:
nothing you ever decided—moving from the East to the
Midwest, taking a promotion, turning another one down—
none of it seemed to trouble her. We're grand, she'd say, to
almost anything. There were times it drove you nuts, you
know that, and she must have, too, but she just did whatever
it was she did, and everything turned out well. When the
boys came along, she'd quite suddenly become beautiful; it
had lasted four or five years, and you'd been worried, seeing
the way other men looked at her and knowing you weren't
that much of a prize. She hadn't seemed to know that,
though—that you were pretty ordinary—and as she got
older, she went back to looking ordinary, but nothing had

ever changed, really. You'd complain to her, about work or the boys or the house or even about her, and she'd just keep going, and show you how that was done without you really noticing. She had been eager; you can't remember her when she didn't have news to tell, a plan to consider, something she thought you might want to try, something she was looking forward to. She talked too much, and indulged the boys, and volunteered you for things, but for forty years she'd been all the company you'd needed, and you do not know how to go on.

You have the distinct feeling that your hair is sticking out over your ears and making you look as foolish as you feel, so you smooth it down before you walk out of the sitting room and into the little entryway and look out—for crying out loud, looking out the door before you close it is something everybody does—and see the Traveller woman walking away.

It's not like you ever had a conversation with her; it's not like she was friendly in any way, but you know you'll miss her coming to the door. You'll miss putting things into the bag. Until right now you didn't even know you'd been enjoying expecting her.

Maybe she's going home. If she is, she's heading in the right direction, toward what people still call the Bishop's

Field, although long before you got here, it had been paved and provided with amenities, as they call electric and sewer hookups, for the Travellers. It's an official halting site for them, a hard stand, a place they can camp for a while without being hassled. You've seen a bit of it from the road, glancing up between the gateposts; you've noticed the washing hung out or the dogs racing and ramping.

For just a second, you imagine following her along the streets and then up the rise to that hard stand, the gravel under your shoes. You don't know her name, but you've pretended it might be Molly Connor, and you've even pretended that you might irritate Róisín by saying, Molly Connor stopped by yesterday, so she'd say, Molly Connor? and you'd say, You know—that Traveller woman.

You know what people say about Travellers, these Irish Gypsies who travel around in small camping trailers, called caravans, and stop by the side of the road, when and where they please, for as long as they feel like it, or until somebody forces them to move on. Róisín calls them tinkers, which seems to be a slur, and says they're dirty thieves; certainly mending pots and pans is ancient history. Her husband, Michael, says they'll steal your gates and gutters and sell them back to you; Mrs. Duggan in the shop claims their old men marry girls as young as thirteen, and the men beat the women, and the children are put to begging.

On the other hand, you've also heard they're fierce

Catholics with strong, stable families, loyal beyond belief to one another, and you read somewhere that they have rules about cooking as strict as kosher Jews. Not long ago a fellow in Taylor's pub claimed that when they get rich, however they manage it, they build themselves fine big houses, and then leave the comfort of those houses and let them stand empty most of the year, while they crowd into their little caravans and go back on the road. Michael's grandnephew Shane said once that every Traveller boy has his own horse. "You see them tied with rope outside the caravans," Shane said, and then he shrugged. "I wish I could be a Traveller, with my own horse, and be wild." Once upon a time, they must have actually traveled in the gaudy horse-drawn wagons that sometimes show up on postcards, but you're sure that people who live in houses never found these people quaint.

The woman walking away doesn't look quaint, or wild, but she's walking away, and you've got to shut the door and go back in and deal with Róisín, because the fact is that you're not wild either, and you're not a kid: you're just a mess. You can't stand to use your own bathroom because Mary's nightgown and robe are still hanging there, and you can't bring yourself to move them. Most nights you fall asleep on the couch with the television on; you haven't slept in your own bed since the boys left a few days after the funeral. This disaster today—you thought it was part of the solution, grabbing Mary's clothes out of the closet to offer to the Traveller woman, but you can see it's just part of the problem: you can't get a grip.

The truth is that the house, empty, ignores you, and that makes it hard to be in it. So you spend a lot of time in the garden, and walk with the dog twice a day now, long walks along the bay; once a week you take a taxi up the hill to the cemetery, and tend Mary's parents' grave, as you have for years, and any day now you're going to start laying out the garden you designed for Mary's. Your son Kevin was so sure you couldn't learn to cook you haven't bothered—you eat supper out, and sometimes you stop into Taylor's afterward for a whiskey or two and the chance to listen to people talk. Some evenings you have three, and some evenings you want another after you get home. You've considered not keeping any in the house; those sad Irish drunks everybody used to laugh at are sometimes in your mind, and they don't seem near as funny now as they used to.

You meant to guard against letting things go, but you don't know—obviously—just what Mary did to "keep the house" for the five years the two of you lived in this one, or to keep the other houses all those years before you retired and she talked you into coming here to live. You don't exactly know what would constitute "letting it go," but you know for sure you're doing that.

And, apparently, worse than that; otherwise Róisín wouldn't be in there, and you wouldn't be out here, wishing you didn't have to go in there, wishing you had a little caravan parked here that you could just hop into and drive away, leave all this behind.

Which, you remind yourself, you can't do. You don't have that little caravan, and you don't have anywhere to go.

Of course, you do have somewhere you can go: you can go back to the States. You're not Irish, you don't particularly like this house, your sons live in America, you're getting old, and you're falling apart. You can walk back in there, and when she demands her explanation, you can just tell her you've made your decision, you'll be clearing everything out and putting the house on the market and going back where you belong. Rent an apartment, hire a damned cleaning service. Take up golf. Go live in Florida like everybody else and die alone. Even as you shut the door, you know better. You can't even make yourself open Mary's bathroom drawer; how are you going to call a goddamn real estate agent? You can't even stay mad for as long as it takes to get from the front door back to the sitting room—four steps, maximum.

Róisín is pulling hangers out of the clothes on the couch, and she doesn't look up. "I'll just take these things along to the Curiosity Shop. There's no point in giving them to those people—they'll toss them out and nobody get the use of them. Those women, they take advantage terrible." She's arranging the hangers neatly on the seat of your chair as she takes them out of the necks of the clothes. She shakes her head. "You've no idea," she says, and picks up a shirt and folds it, and then holds it to her face for a second. When she lowers it, she says—and her voice is shy—"There's a bit of her smell still."

You stand there, vague and embarrassed, with no sense of Mary's smell at all, but with the surprising sense that Róisín sounded like her, just for a second there.

"I've had it in my mind to come and get them," Róisín says, completely herself again. "I think I've a big sack in the car they'll fit into, and I'll take them round one day next week." Now she does glance at you, quickly, and she actually smiles.

And the doorbell rings.

There you both are, with stupid half grins on your faces.

"I'll get that," you say.

"If it's that woman come back . . ." Róisín says, almost a whisper, and you see that she's actually afraid.

"I'm sure," you say, vaguely, turning, but you do go slowly enough that you can see before you get to the door that it isn't the Traveller woman, but a fairly little boy, so you open the door. "Yes?"

He runs the edge of his hand beneath his nose before he speaks, and then he doesn't meet your eyes but looks past your shoulder. "Me sister says she left a bag of food here," he says.

The comfort that starts in your chest is like you used to feel when Mary said something perfectly ordinary after you'd quarreled, a kind of easing in your chest—maybe she'll go on coming to the door now and then—and you smile, you're about to agree that yes, she did, and you'll get it for him, but behind you Róisín says, "The cheek! There's nothing for you in this house—you go along!"

The boy glances at the ground, sniffs, digs his finger quickly in his ear, and looks up again. "She says she left a jumper here, too," he says.

"You scamp!" Róisín says, and she steps past you and reaches for him, but he dances back, grinning. "You clear out, you bold boy, before I get the gards in here!"

"A gray jumper, she said," the boy cries, "old as you and baggy as him!" and then he spins and pelts away down the road, crowing wildly.

You make the tea, because clearly Róisín shouldn't be trusted at the moment with boiling water.

"I know that boy," she says, for the fifth or sixth time, "I know him, and I'll have the gards moving him along on Shop Street, you see if I don't, you just see if I don't—bawl-

ing 'Molly Malone' at the top of his lungs for the tourists—
you just see." She keeps walking back and forth from one
end of the table to the other, moving the chairs a bit and
then moving them back. "Filthy little thief—the cheek of
those ones! The cheek!"

You pour the tea into two blue mugs and set them on the
table. "Have some tea," you say.

She stops then and faces you, gripping the back of a chair
with both hands, and it occurs to you that something is
wrong with this picture: her face is red, and yours isn't. She's
mad, and you're not.

"You should have collared him, Lyle—you should have
known he was a dirty tinker sent by that nasty woman! You
should have grabbed the little knacker and taught him a lesson!"

You meet her eyes. "Róisín," you say. "I'm too . . . baggy."

"Laugh!" she says. "Go on—laugh, but they'll be back,
mind what I say!"

You're not laughing, but you are grinning. You can't help
yourself, and she probably can't either: she picks the chair
up an inch off the floor and jams it back down and says,
"Drink your own feckin' tea!"

For a woman nearly seventy, she moves fast, and slams the
door behind her with remarkable vigor.

You sit there a minute, grinning like a fool and listening to
the house. It's quiet. It's waiting.

So you say, "Might as well."

Lady, who has wisely spent the last half hour in her crate in the laundry room, comes out and sits just past the kitchen threshold. You meet her eyes, and shrug.

Half the clothes are folded, a dark blue skirt on top. You pick it up carefully and see how it was done—lengthwise in half, then the other way twice. It seems simple enough, and when you fold the next skirt, a green one, it looks much like the one Róisín did, and you put it on the pile.

When the heap has become three fairly neat stacks, you go upstairs and find an empty box in the guest room closet, and carry it downstairs and put the clothes into it. They don't quite fill it, so you go back up to Mary's closet and get the rest of the things—jackets and blouses—and do your best to get them neatly in on top, and you close the box.

Then you go back up, to the bathroom, and you just pull out the whole drawer from her side of the sink and dump it into the wastebasket without looking at anything, drop her toothbrush and hairbrush in there, too, and lift the bag out. And, yes, you have to look yourself in the eye in the mirror first, but you take the nightgown and bathrobe off the hook on the back of the door, and you don't hold them to your face, you don't check to see if they have her smell about them still: you put them into the trash bag, tie it up, and take it down and out the back door to the garbage can.

When you come back in, you put the box in the entryway, and then you get the bag of food from the sitting room and hang it back on the hook in the laundry room.

You refill the kettle and plug it in, and while you're waiting, you get one of the lawn chairs your son bought for you out of the laundry room. To Lady, who has stayed with you every step, you say, "I think I'll take my tea alfresco. Care to join me?"

She follows you out the back door and watches while you unfold the chair, and go back in and make your tea, and come back out and sit down.

Mary should come now with the other mug, and stand near you, looking at the flowers. You can see her as she was when you first met her, wearing a soft blouse and a dark skirt, her hair done up somehow, but the Mary who lived here with you is somehow there as well, stout and gray-haired. "Róisín and her temper," she says.

It seems to you that everything that has just happened in the house has to do with Mary, with meeting her for the first time, with loving her. You know she isn't here beside you, tapping her fingernails against the mug's side. "The lad was cheeky," she says. "But it was an ugly jumper." She sips the tea. "She'll get over being put out," she says.

You sit for a while longer, knowing she's right: Róisín's temper, like your own, is a quick, hot thing, and it's easier to laugh off being called baggy than being called ugly.

Mary laughs, and for the first time her death seems to be past, as her life does, too. All that uproar and shouting in the house, the Traveller woman's scuffing—they seem to have cleared the house, and made of Mary a ghost that can come back.

You set your mug on the grass and take the dog into your lap. The ground is too soft, and the legs of the chair are sinking in a little, but it's pleasant out here, the flowers look good. The Irish don't tend to sit out as much as Americans do, but you don't see why you shouldn't. You could put down paving stones here, make a small patio. Make it about six by eight, set the pavers maybe half an inch apart so the grass will grow between them. You pet the dog's smooth, small head, and you start calculating how many pavers you'll need.